SPY DOG

Andrew Cope was born in Derby in 1966. He is a teacher and writer, and a huge fan of Derby County Football Club. He really does have a dog called Lara, who has one sticky-up ear and came from the RSPCA, but he's not sure if she is actually a highly trained secret agent. Andrew lives with his wife and two children. This is his first book.

2/30

SPY DOG

ANDREW COPE

Illustrated by Chris Mould

PUFFIN

PUFFIN BOOKS

Published by the Penguin Group
Penguin Books Ltd, 80 Strand, London WC2R 0RL, England
Penguin Group (USA) Inc., 375 Hudson Street, New York, New York 10014, USA
Penguin Group (Canada), 90 Eglinton Avenue East, Suite 700, Toronto, Ontario,
Canada M4P 2Y3 (a division of Pearson Penguin Canada Inc.)
Penguin Ireland, 25 St Stephen's Green, Dublin 2, Ireland
(a division of Penguin Books Ltd)
Penguin Group (Australia), 250 Camberwell Road, Camberwell, Victoria 3124,
Australia (a division of Pearson Australia Group Pty Ltd)
Penguin Books India Pvt Ltd, 11 Community Centre, Panchsheel Park,
New Delhi – 110 017, India
Penguin Group (NZ), cnr Airborne and Rosedale Roads, Albany, Auckland 1310,
New Zealand (a division of Pearson New Zealand Ltd)
Penguin Books (South Africa) (Pty) Ltd, 24 Sturdee Avenue, Rosebank,
Johannesburg 2196, South Africa

Penguin Books Ltd, Registered Offices: 80 Strand, London WC2R 0RL, England

www.penguin.com

First published 2005
This edition produced for The Book People Ltd,
Hall Wood Avenue, Haydock, St Helens, WA11 9UL

1

Text copyright © Andrew Cope, 2005
Illustrations copyright © Chris Mould, 2005
All rights reserved

The moral right of the author and illustrator has been asserted

Set in Bembo
Made and printed in England by Clays Ltd, St Ives plc

British Library Cataloguing in Publication Data
A CIP catalogue record for this book is available from the British Library

ISBN-13: 978-0-141-33672-5

www.greenpenguin.co.uk

Mixed Sources
Product group from well-managed
forests and other controlled sources
www.fsc.org Cert no. SA-COC-1592
© 1996 Forest Stewardship Council

FSC

Penguin Books is committed to a sustainable future
for our business, our readers and our planet.
The book in your hands is made from paper
certified by the Forest Stewardship Council.

For my favourite daughter

Thanks to:

Greg
For your expert opinion. I took your advice and improved the manuscript. I bow to your genius.

Hayley, Marc, Lauren, Will and Thomas
You all read the draft manuscript, liked it and spurred me on. I changed the bits you didn't like.

Mr Bell and the Year 3 class from Melbourne Junior School (2003)
Mr Bell for reading it to the class, and all the pupils for listening so politely.

Ju
For the crazy ideas. Gadgets, there just had to be gadgets . . . it was so obvious. I think the gadgets swung it.

Lucy, Rosemary, Sarah and Shannon
For choosing to go with *Spy Dog*. Without you, the manuscript would be gathering dust in the attic! Massive thanks are due.

Lou
For patience, support, encouragement and ideas, particularly on the umpteenth rewrite when the going got especially tough.

The RSPCA, Abbey Street, Derby
For letting us adopt Lara, without whom there would have been no inspiration.

Contents

1. *A Brush with Death*

The man with the gun was prowling nearby. Lara couldn't see him but she could smell him. She still had the taste of his flesh in her mouth. She crouched, absolutely still, half hidden in the undergrowth.

A twig cracked underfoot. 'Where are you, dog?' he cursed. 'I have a little something for you.'

Yes, and that little something is a bullet, thought Lara as she adjusted her position in readiness to leap at the man.

He came into view, the gun held out in front of him, walking carefully, occasionally turning round full circle. His clothes were torn, his arms were scratched and his leg was bleeding badly, souvenirs of his encounter with the dog he was now determined to shoot.

Lara remained still, controlling her breathing and the urge to run. The man came closer. He must have seen her. It would only be a matter of time. *Wait for the right moment and I might live to fight another day.* Now, just a couple of metres away, she could see the barrel of the gun. She could smell that it had recently been used.

It's now or never. Go! Lara leapt from her

hiding place, surprising the man and sinking her teeth into his arm. He yelled in pain and dropped the weapon.

The dog sprinted away. *I must get out of this wood. Just run and don't look back.* She couldn't see the man, but obviously he had found his gun. She heard a shot, and a bullet thudded into a nearby tree. She ran faster, zigzagging out of the way as more shots were fired. An empty Coke can jumped high into the air as a stray bullet hit it. The noise was enough to wake her . . .

Lara leapt to her feet. At first she wasn't sure where she was. There was no wood, no undergrowth and no gun. Instead there was a concrete floor, a water bowl and some iron bars . . . She quickly recovered her senses.

Lara was in the safety of the RSPCA. She had been dreaming of her brush with death five days ago.

2. The Waiting Game

Lara had spent the last five days studying ordinary dogs. She had resisted the temptation to choose just any old owner, although the prospect of a quick escape from the RSPCA was almost overwhelming. She was following orders. *I must choose a family. Be patient. I will know when the right owners come along.*

Lara noticed that the pretty dogs with good manners tended to stay only a few hours, whereas the uglier ones with gruff barks stayed a lot longer. In fact, some she had spoken to had been in their cages for months. *A bit of a shame that humans choose according to looks*, she thought. *Maybe I can help one of the long-serving dogs get adopted?*

She decided to help Bruce in cell

thirty-four. He had been caged for nearly six months and Lara noticed that his size and his energy put off a lot of potential owners. Even worse, he got so excited when people came round that he jumped up at the bars and howled like a wolf. Yet when nobody was around Bruce was the nicest, softest dog on the row. At exercise time, Lara took him to one side. *Look here, Bruce,* she barked. *Have you ever considered why you've been here for six months?*

Bruce wasn't the brightest. He hadn't really considered very much at all, only that he was desperate to have a family and that the more he tried the worse it got.

Lara had coached him in basic relaxation and manners. The very next day she was delighted to see him taking deep breaths and composing himself as a lady approached his cage. *Good lad, Brucey,* she thought. *No barking or jumping up. Keep it cool.* Then, as per the plan, Bruce lay down and rolled over for a tummy tickle, and Lara watched as the lady stopped at cage thirty-four and patted his belly. Lara knew that Bruce was fighting his urge to bounce and howl. She was willing him on. *Fight the urge, lad. Stay strong, she thought. Sad eyes, Bruce . . . do your sad eyes . . . like we practised.* Right on cue, Bruce got to his feet and sat before the lady, offering his paw through the bars. He did his sad eyes, just as they'd rehearsed, and Lara saw the lady's face break into a pitying smile. Lara punched the air in delight as the lady asked for cage thirty-four to be opened. *No bouncing.* Take some *deep breaths, Brucey,* she thought. *Don't blow your chance now. Remember the final move.* At exactly the right moment, Bruce planted a big wet lick across the lady's face and sealed his adoption. Lara

led the howls of delight as Bruce was led away, bouncing with excitement.

Thanks for the advice, Lara, he barked. *I owe you one. See you on the outside.*

Bruce's departure left fifty-three dogs at the RSPCA. Lara was staggered at the variety on offer: cute and cuddly, large and smelly, short-haired, long-eared, pedigrees, mongrels, sleek and beautiful, fat and ugly, puppies, fully grown dogs, some smiling, some sad – but all with one thing in common: they longed for a loving home.

The Cook family pulled up outside the

RSPCA, bright and early on a Saturday morning. The back doors of the car swung open and three children bolted up the steps and burst into the RSPCA office. Mum and Dad emerged more slowly. Dad stretched and Mum was still wiping the sleep from her eyes. The children had been so excited about choosing a dog that they'd been up half the night.

Dad explained to the lady behind the counter that they would like to choose a family pet. The lady smiled and pointed to the wooden gate. 'Go through that gate into the yard,' she told them. 'We have a wonderful selection of dogs for you to choose from.'

Mum, Dad, Ben, Sophie and Ollie went through the gate to choose their dog. Little did they suspect that actually it was Lara who would choose them.

3. The Incredible Whistling Dog

The Cooks were a perfect family for any of the dogs but, unfortunately for the abandoned animals, they could only choose one. Mum and Dad worked full-time, so they were relying on Gran, who lived across the road, to look after the new pet during the day.

Ben, Sophie and Ollie ran up and down past the cages. Dogs of all shapes and sizes tried to win their affections, rolling over for tummy tickles, barking wildly, lying forlornly, shaking paws – each dog had its own tactic for being chosen. Each tried to outdo the others.

Sophie rushed between the cages, shrieking with glee at the different animals. 'Look at this one, Dad,' she squealed. 'It's got brown, floppy ears and sad eyes. If we took it home, we could cheer it up. And this one's jumping up at me. I think he loves me.'

'He's a she,' noted Dad, reading from the notice above the cage. 'Her name's Lizzy and she's already been reserved. See what others you can find.'

'Here are some tiny puppies,' cooed Sophie's younger brother. 'Look at them, they're all cute and cuddly. We could take all four and then they'd never be lonely.'

Dad calmed him. 'Just the one, Ollie. If we can find a mutt we think we can all love, we'll take it. If not, we'll have to try again another day.'

As far as Sophie's older brother was concerned, there would be no other day. Ben had permission to choose a dog, so choose a dog he would – today. He had nagged his parents for the last two years and they'd always said, 'Not until you're old enough to look after a dog properly.'

'When will that be?' he'd pleaded.

'Probably when you reach double figures,' Dad had said, and the children had been counting down to today, Ben's tenth birthday. Mum and Dad smiled as their three children galloped to and fro, as excitable as the dogs themselves.

Lara was no ordinary dog. She listened, taking it all in and playing it cool. She had calculated that the older children, Ben and Sophie, would be the ones who would sway any decision. If she could win them over, then she would be going home with the Cooks tonight.

On Sophie's first pass, Lara tried the sympathy vote, lying in her classic doggie pose with her head on her front paws, looking slightly sad, putting on her long face with droopy eyes. *It worked for Bruce*, she thought as Sophie sprinted straight past without so much as a second glance. Panic set in. *The sad eyes haven't worked*. Lara was worried that if Sophie made it to the end cage, she would fall in love with a twelve-week-old puppy called Toby. She couldn't allow that to happen. A new tactic was needed, and quick.

Lara sprang to her feet and sniffed beyond the bars of her cage. She could smell Ollie

close by, but she couldn't see him. She suspected he was scratching the tummy of a basset hound, four doors down. She could hear him murmuring about how he would take care of this cute animal when it came to his house. Horror upon horror, her chance was slipping away. *I can't stand another day here. This is my chosen family.* Ben was scratching the head of Jasmine in cage one. Lara had to act, and act now. Fortunately she had been highly trained for just such a moment – now was the time to put her superior talents to good use. Without hesitation, Lara stood on her hind legs, put her left forepaw in her doggy mouth and, clear as day, whistled to

Ollie. The other dogs fell momentarily silent. *What was that?* barked Rex, an Alsatian of three weeks' residence.

Came from that new dog in cage eight, replied Sabre, his Labrador pal from three cages down. *But dogs can't whistle.*

How wrong they were. Lara had whistled perfectly, so it came out as a shrill, football-referee type of whistle, making everyone turn round and look, scratching their heads, wondering where the sound came from.

Ollie came running up to cage eight. 'Was that you, doggie?' he enquired innocently.

Lara barked excitedly. *Yes, yes, of course it was. Now go and get your brother and sister,* thought Lara, frustrated that she could understand words but couldn't speak them. Standing on her hind legs, she pointed towards Ben, stabbing her paw wildly in his direction.

'Doggies aren't supposed to be able to whistle,' said Ollie matter-of-factly. 'They bark and bite and chase cats, but they can't whistle . . . or point.'

This one can, thought Lara, still upright on her hind legs. She jabbed her paw more wildly, this time towards Sophie, knowing that she was getting closer to the cute puppy at the end of the row. *For goodness sake, go and fetch your sister. Can't you see I've chosen you?*

'Sophie, can dogs whistle?' shouted Ollie to his older sister.

'Ollie, you pea brain, of course they can't. Don't they teach you anything at nursery? They woof and whine and fetch sticks and things, but they can't whistle,' chirped his sister as she scampered towards the end of the row. 'Hey, Mummy, come and look at these cute brown puppies,' she called, chancing on the final cage.

Lara was now on red alert. If her plan were

to work, if she were to go home with her chosen family tonight, she would have to take drastic action. While Ollie watched, she stood on her hind legs, put her paw in her mouth and let out another shrill whistle, not quite as loud as the previous one, but pretty ear-splitting all the same. Ollie watched, open-mouthed. 'Ben . . . Sophie . . .' he gasped, 'come and look at this whistling dog.'

That was how Lara caught Ollie's attention, who in turn caught Sophie's attention, who chatted it through with Ben, who worked on Mum and Dad, who finally told the lady from the RSPCA that they would like to take Lara home as their new family pet.

'Ollie says she can whistle,' joked Dad to the lady behind the RSPCA counter.

'Oh, good,' replied the lady, going along with the joke. 'Perhaps he will teach her to sing too!' The adults thought this was very funny.

Lara listened intently to the banter. *Stupid woman*, she thought. *I may be able to whistle tunes, read music and play the piano, but even spy dogs can't sing.*

4. *Following Orders*

In fact 'Lara' wasn't Lara's name at all. She didn't have a name, just a reference number, GM451, given to her by the British government. The silver disc round her neck said 'LARA' in bold letters, but this actually stood for 'Licensed Assault and Rescue Animal'. Lara was an experiment. This outwardly cuddly mongrel was, in fact, a highly trained special agent, bred by the British Secret Service for use on dangerous missions throughout the world. On her last mission Lara had escaped from a dangerous criminal who, she was sure, would be hunting her down. Her orders were clear: if separated from her handlers, she had to pretend to be a normal dog, allow herself to be captured by the RSPCA and secure herself a nice home with a family. She should simply melt into the background and wait for the Secret Service to track her down.

Before she had picked the Cook family, Lara had been singled out by several possible owners. She hadn't really liked the look of any of them. The closest she'd come to adoption was by a fat man wearing a football shirt that wasn't big enough to cover his tummy. As a result, his hairy belly flopped over his belt buckle like a saggy bag of dough. A cigarette hung from the corner of his mouth as though it were a permanent fixture. Lara willed him to keep walking, but he stopped outside her cage. *Just my luck*, she thought. *If he adopts me, there's no chance of any exercise at all.* She watched as he stuck a fat finger up his nose and rummaged around, finding something and examining it closely before adding it to the collection on his shirt. Lara decided that she definitely didn't want to choose him as her new owner. The problem was, he seemed very keen on her.

'How old's this one, love?' he asked the RSPCA warden, pointing to Lara.

'We think she's about three,' replied the woman. 'She's a good-natured bitch, brought in on Tuesday. We found her wandering down the middle of the road just outside the kennels, almost as if she wanted to be spotted and brought in.'

Of course I did, thought Lara, *that's all part of my orders.*

'Is she house-trained?' enquired the man.

Lara was slightly puzzled by this one. *What does he mean 'house-trained'? I'm trained to break into houses and rescue people. I'm trained to cook and I can do basic DIY and am useful to have around the house. I bet that's what he means by 'house-trained'.*

'We think so,' explained the lady. 'She's very clean and is a lovely lady. Very well mannered and quite intelligent.'

Only 'quite intelligent', thought Lara indignantly. *How many languages can you speak? Can you defuse a bomb? Can you play the trombone? I bet you can't do the* Times *crossword in under ten minutes or answer all the questions in Trivial Pursuit like I can.* 'Quite intelligent' *indeed – the cheek of it. Super intelligent more like!*

Lara was tempted to show off just how intelligent she really was. It ran through her mind that if she stood up, danced and whistled 'How much is that doggie in the window?', like she'd been trained to do, that it would make the woman eat her words. But no, she was a professional and her orders were clear. A whistling, dancing dog would hardly melt into the background. More likely the TV cameras would be here within the hour, and her cover would be blown.

She continued to play the dumb dog, but the problem was that this dumb human seemed to think he was compatible with this dumb dog. There was only one thing for it: Lara put into practice her well-rehearsed 'flea bag' routine in a determined attempt to fend off this potential owner. First she composed herself carefully. Then all of a sudden she began to scratch her ears, then her body – a demented scratching accompanied by a crazy face and

a strange, howling noise. She became a frenzy of doggie limbs, all scratching at the same time. Then she ran round in circles until she was completely dizzy and staggered about in her cage as if she were drunk. Then back to the frenzied scratching part. Suddenly she stopped and sat, one ear up, one down, with a big, satisfied doggy smile that said, 'Choose me now if you dare!'

The football-shirted man watched quietly. Lara's performance caused him too to start scratching, his stubby fingers delving into deep, sweaty crevices. His mind was thinking of fleas. He nervously picked some fluff out of his overhanging belly button, pulled the pants out of the crack in his bottom and reviewed his options.

SCRATCH

'Perhaps I need a dog that's definitely been house-trained,' he considered aloud, and sauntered off to the next cage.

Lara spied him later in the RSPCA office, now with a small bulldog in tow. *Give it a football shirt and it would look exactly like him.* She smiled to herself.

Several other people came close to choosing Lara, but she managed to put them off until eventually she decided on the Cooks.

As Dad filled in the paperwork and paid a donation into the RSPCA box, Lara felt a twinge of sadness for the brown puppy that the Cooks would have chosen if she hadn't put her whistling plan into action. She hoped the puppy would find himself a happy home; thinking about it, he was cute, and she was sure he would be OK. In fact, she hoped all the RSPCA dogs would find nice homes to go to, even if they were, in her opinion, a bit thick. *No, that isn't fair, it's just that they are ordinary dogs who haven't had the benefit of my intensive learning programme. They're just normal, it's me that's special. If I sit tight and wait to be rescued, I'll soon be back to a life of adventure.*

5. *Spy School for Beginners*

Lara was pleased to have finally chosen her new owners. The cramped surroundings of the RSPCA had been quite a contrast to her spy-school days. Lara couldn't remember exactly how it had all come about, but she could recall being spotted at an early age and accepted on to Phase One of Professor Cortex's spy dog training programme. Her earliest memory was of the police breaking down the door and gaining entry into the flat. Her owner had been too ill to look after himself and she had been helping him out, going on errands and doing chores around the house. The police had been so impressed with Lara's skills that they'd wanted to keep her for themselves. But Professor Cortex stepped in, and both owner and dog were taken into care – the old man into a home and Lara to spy school.

She had been only a few months old, the youngest of the dogs by far. She remembered the others, the most intelligent of her species. She recalled how ordinary she'd made them look, capable of outsmarting them in every category.

The professor's 'learning lab' had always been spotlessly clean and superbly organized. The animals were very well looked after and each had a reference number rather than a name. The professor wasn't one for first names. The animals were fed well and took regular exercise. In fact, they were in peak condition, having completed assault courses and cross-country runs. Each animal had a comfortable cage to live in, with a TV, stereo and bed. The professor always had a special treat for the dogs, often containing a bubbling formula he had been working on. 'You are what you eat' was one of his favourite sayings. He added extra vitamins, minerals and secret formulae to everything, even to his own food, to maximize the workings of the brain.

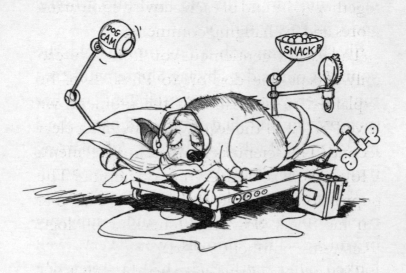

As a result, all the animals in the lab were far more intelligent than average. But he was looking for one that had the potential to be head and shoulders above all the others.

Lara's early days at spy school had been boring. Everything was too easy. She went along with the pack for the first week. She sniffed out the right ball, chased the pretend baddie, found the hidden weapons and completed the cross-country run. *Boring or what?* she thought as the other dogs wagged excitedly at the praise they were receiving. Professor Cortex and his team huddled together at the end of each activity, comparing scores and exchanging comments.

'Ladies and gentlemen, you know we can only accept one dog on to Phase Two,' he explained to his team. 'At the moment, we have PX772 in the lead with MK936 a clear second.' The scientists nodded in agreement. 'How's the black-and-white one doing? The puppy. You know, the one with odd ears?' He ran his finger down the checklist of dogs. 'Reference number GM451.'

They must be talking about me, thought Lara, her sticky-up ear standing even higher as she listened in on the conversation.

'Not too bad, Professor,' explained one of the men in white coats. 'She's doing everything we ask but seems a bit bored by it all. She keeps yawning, and the strange thing is, when she yawns, she puts her paw over her mouth, human style. Weird or what, sir?'

The professor shook his head. He had no time for under-performing animals. He was only interested in super beasts. 'We can only accept one,' he reminded them. 'It has to be the right one. We can't have one that's bored, can we?'

Well, give me a proper challenge and I wouldn't be, thought Lara. *I mean, come on Prof. For goodness' sake, give us a proper test. What about some reading or writing for a start?* Lara knew this was way beyond the other dogs, but she was proud of the fact that she could hold a pencil in her mouth and scribble. *Not bad for a puppy, she thought, but I want to learn letters and numbers like humans use. I know I could do it if someone got me started.*

The professor had trained all sorts of animals for the British Secret Service. His special laboratory held monkeys, rats, mice, birds, lizards, ferrets and pigs. The pigs thought themselves superior. Lara couldn't speak Pig, but she could tell by their attitude that they thought they were the best. Sure, they were bright – but put them out in the sun for too long and their backs got burnt like crispy bacon. *Not very useful on outdoor missions – and besides, pigs can never fit in like dogs can. Imagine a spy pig!* She chuckled to herself. *It just won't happen.* The ferrets were OK, but when the pressure was on they made for the nearest trouser leg. Cats were quite

intelligent, but too lazy. Parrots could talk but not understand. Monkeys weren't as bright as the professor had hoped, plus they couldn't slip into situations unnoticed. He had come to the conclusion that his chosen animal would have to be a dog. After three decades of effort, the professor was pinning his last hope on man's best friend. He looked at the twelve dogs sitting before him, all their tails wagging hard, all with a chance of being chosen for Phase Two. The professor knew all their backgrounds: four had won dog shows, three were top-performing police dogs, two were highly intelligent guide dogs, two were prize-winning sheepdogs, and one, the youngest, had been rescued from an old man's flat.

'One of you will be chosen as top dog,' announced the professor. 'Our first ever Licensed Assault and Rescue Animal. If only you could understand, you'd know how important it is to be chosen.'

Eleven of the pack wagged furiously. The man was talking to them and, although they couldn't understand him, he sounded nice. The black-and-white puppy understood every word. *Important, eh?* she thought. *I think I'll play it cool until you tell me more.*

The professor and his team set them a series of tasks; he called it his 'Canine Olympics'. Lara remembered the time when each dog was issued with a special computer. Each key had a picture on it, and when the professor held up an image the dogs were instructed to press the correct button. First he held up a picture of a bone. *Boring or what?* sighed Lara, rolling her eyes and pressing her bone button. She leant over to help PX772, who hadn't a clue what was going on. *Look, a bone*, she woofed, pointing to the professor's picture. *So find the button with the bone . . . Here, look. And press it, like this. Simple.*

Lara ignored her own
computer, preferring
instead to try and coach PX772.
As a result he was top of the class.
She knew he was a show dog, top of
his breed, but to Lara he was just a yappy,
jumpy-up kind of dog, with no talent for
anything except doing somersaults. But the
professor and his expert team were
impressed. They fussed over PX772 as if he
were really special. 'Excellent score,'
enthused the professor. 'You have a clear
lead.' PX772 sat and wagged, polishing the
wooden floor, clueless as to what was going
on around him.

*

Lara didn't like showing off. She knew she was the cleverest dog there but hated to be big-headed. It was the final activity of week three that brought her to the professor's attention. The animal-research team had organized a mountain rescue. The professor gathered the dogs together and tried his best to explain. 'See these hills,' he said, pointing to the peaks behind him. 'There is a wounded man somewhere. Obviously not really wounded, we are pretending. You must sniff him out and raise the alarm. Understand?' Eleven dogs wagged furiously, not understanding a word. Lara sat still, taking it all in, wondering whether she could be bothered. The professor held out a shirt for the dogs to sniff, then off they sprinted, noses to the ground, barking wildly. Except Lara. She sniffed the shirt and sat for a while, watching the others scampering into the distance.

'Go on, GM451. The others will beat you if you don't hurry,' urged Professor Cortex.

Lara raised an eyebrow in a couldn't-care-less kind of way. *Not necessarily, Prof.*, she thought. *They might all have gone off in the wrong direction. Remember, 'fools rush in . . .' A plan. That's what's needed.* She watched as the professor and his team went back into their office. She wandered over to the window and sat for a while longer, listening to their conversation.

'Agent W's going to head off to Callow Rock,' explained the professor. 'That's a good ten kilometres away. It will take the dogs ages to find him. Someone put the kettle on. He'll radio in when they've found him.'

Callow Rock, thought Lara. *Sounds like a hill, but I wonder which one?* She wandered off, her head full of ideas but with no particular plan. The heavens opened and she took refuge in a bus shelter. *Think, Lara, think. There must be a way to find Callow Rock.*

Right on cue, a red bus pulled up and a passenger struggled on. 'Callow Top return, please,' she heard him say.

Lara's ears pricked up and her mind whirred into action. *I guess Callow Rock must be somewhere near Callow Top? It's got to be worth a go.* She tried to sneak on to the bus but the driver would have none of it, shooing her off. *Fair enough*, she thought, *I'll have to do this the hard way*, and she began to chase the bus.

Callow Top was a very big hill. The bus crawled up the incline and round the corners, the engine screaming and black smoke belching from its exhaust. Lara sprinted for all she was worth, ears tight to her head and tongue flopping. Her chest was heaving and her muscles aching as she approached the top of Callow Hill. *Is this is a hill or a mountain?* she gasped as the bus pulled over and the passenger got off. Lara trotted across the road and heard the driver commenting to the passenger that there was another of those black-and-white dogs. 'Identical to the one at the bottom of the hill,' she heard him say.

Identical in every way, thought Lara, *except this one's worn out!*

The bus pulled away and started down the other side of the hill. Lara sat and sucked some oxygen into her lungs, surprising herself at the speed of her recovery. *Looks like the professor's fitness programme is paying off.* There was no sign of the other dogs or the man she was supposed to be rescuing. Lara

stood on her hind legs and sniffed the wind.
There was a faint smell to her left so she
trotted towards the cliff edge. She looked
down, and there on a small ledge below was
a man. By the smell of him he was the man
she was looking for. *Easy peasy*, she thought.
Top marks for me.

She looked again and noticed that he
wasn't moving. She barked. Nothing. Lara
became a little concerned. Perhaps the man
really was injured? She found a rope in his
rucksack and hooked one end on to a
branch, giving it a tug to test its strength. She
threw the rope down to the ledge and then,
using her teeth, she lowered herself down to

the man and checked him over. There was a large bump on his head and he had what looked like a broken ankle. *I thought he was only supposed to be pretending*, she thought. *If so, this is a very good act!*

Lara reached into the man's pocket and retrieved his walkie-talkie. Her clumsy paws made it difficult, but she managed to press the 'talk' button. She barked three times and released the button.

After a few seconds Professor Cortex replied, 'Agent W, is that you? You sound funny. Over.'

Lara pressed and barked again. *For goodness' sake, Prof., Agent W's out cold, she thought. Come and rescue him.*

The walkie-talkie crackled again. 'Agent W ... Agent W?' replied the professor, a note of urgency rising in his voice. 'Come in, Agent W.'

Come in? What do you mean 'come in'? He can't come anywhere because he's fallen off a cliff! Lara held down the button and whined. *Surely he'll get it this time*, she thought. *As far as I know, Agent W doesn't bark or whine.*

There was a long silence at the other end.

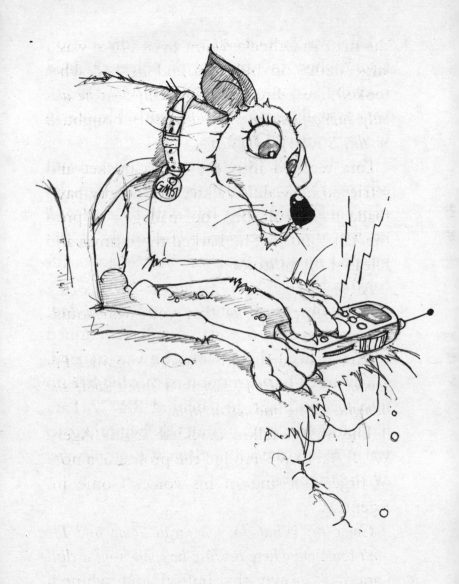

Lara was just about to press the button again when the professor's voice crackled over the airwaves. 'Agent W . . . Agent W . . . we are sending assistance urgently. Please stay where you are. Over and out.'

By the time the Secret Service team arrived, she had done her best to strap the man's ankle and cover him with his coat. *Still no sign of the other dogs*, she thought as she jumped into the back of the van for a lift back to base.

Naturally the professor was astounded: Lara had tracked the man down, summoned help and been there when he was rescued. He awarded her extra points, moving her up into second place, just behind PX772. Lara had enjoyed the day and was beginning to warm to spy school. *Perhaps it is for me after all*, she thought.

6. *Spy School (Advanced)*

The successful mountain rescue had changed Lara's attitude to spy school. *If I'm chosen for Phase Two, I'll get a life of excitement, action and adventure. Think of all the good I could do, all the criminals I could put behind bars and all the fun I could have.* Lara decided to focus her efforts on showing her true talents.

Her first opportunity to shine came that very night. The professor locked up and switched off the light. The dogs settled down for the night. Lara lay on her bed and thought about spy school. She knew the professor and his team would choose just one dog to go forward to the next level of training. She'd heard them talking about it and knew that she was in second place. *I just hope I haven't left it too late.* She nodded off, dreaming of chasing baddies.

Lara woke with a start and glanced at the clock. She hadn't quite mastered telling the time yet, but the big hand was on the twelve and the little hand was on the two. She knew it was very late. She came to her senses and pricked up her ears. The other dogs snored on. One of the farm dogs was particularly noisy, whining and twitching in his sleep, obviously rounding up sheep. *There's the noise again, very faint but getting louder. It sounds like footsteps tiptoeing outside.* Lara cocked her head to listen. Suddenly there was a loud crash and a brick came through the window, glass showering the floor. The dogs all awoke and started yapping. *Calm down, you lot,* barked Lara, trying to concentrate on what was going on. A gloved hand appeared through the broken window and undid the catch. The window swung open and a shadowy figure climbed in. The yapping frenzy increased. Lara stayed calm. *The professor and his team have some very valuable equipment and I bet the data on his computer is worth a fortune.*

The shadow man moved swiftly around the

lab, his boots crunching on the glass. He shone his torch into some of the cages. 'Silence, dogs,' he cursed. 'I'm stealing to order. I only need one of you. In fact, I only need the top dog.' He stepped between the cages until he found the one he was looking for. He fumbled with a bunch of keys and unlocked PX772's cage, before clipping a lead on to his collar and tying the other end to a chair. PX772 sat obediently while the caged dogs barked furiously. As the shadow man moved towards the computer, Lara decided she must take action. *I can't just sit by and let this burglar get away with the professor's hard work, can I?*

She jumped on to her bed and pulled the pillow aside. There was the key to her cage. (She always kept a spare in case of emergencies. *You just never know*, she'd thought as she took it from the professor's pocket.) Lara picked up the key in her mouth and inserted it in the keyhole. She twisted her head and unlocked the cage door, pushing it open with her nose.

The burglar obviously knew what he was after. He didn't want the whole computer, just the information on the hard drive. He unscrewed the computer and got what he had come for. *He's got the top-scoring dog and all the professor's data*, thought Lara. *I can't let him get away with it.*

'Come on, mutt, let's get out of here,' he said to PX772, untying him from the chair.

Not if I can help it, thought Lara. She leapt out of the shadows and sank her teeth into the man's ankle. The burglar cursed and kicked out, dropping the drive. Lara picked the drive up and scurried back into her cage,

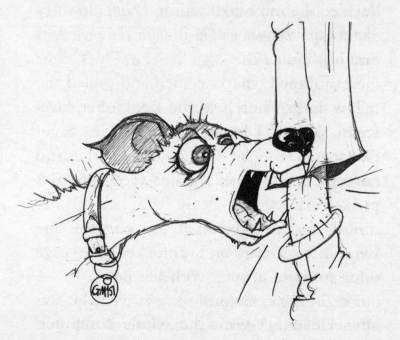

hiding it under her pillow. The man flashed his torch in her direction. 'Give me that hard drive, mutt,' he said. 'It's very valuable.'

Come and get it then, she thought, tempting him into her cage.

The man was wary. He wasn't sure whether Lara would bite him again, so he edged carefully into the cage, feeling his way in the dark. 'Nice puppy,' he soothed, trying to keep himself and the dog calm. 'Give me the disk like a nice pup.'

Lara took her chance and trotted out, leaving him to scrabble under the pillow. By the time he'd pocketed the drive, Lara had carefully closed the cage door and locked it, then swallowed the key.

The burglar watched as she gulped the key down. He was beside himself with rage. 'What . . . How . . .?' he blustered. 'Let me out, you stupid mutt!' he yelled, rattling the bars.

Hang on, thought Lara. *I'm out here and you're locked in the cage, so who's the stupid one?*

Lara barked for the other animals to be quiet. *Everyone, please, the excitement's over. This silly man was trying to rob the professor and steal*

PX772. Let's get some sleep, and we'll sort this mess out in the morning.

The noise subsided and the dogs eventually went back to sleep. All was quiet, except for the noise Lara made as she swept up the mess.

The professor was in bright and early. He lived for his work and was annoyed that sleep had to get in the way. He placed his thumb on the security pad and the door slid open. His eyes widened as he saw Lara helping herself to some cornflakes while the other dogs waited obediently for their breakfast. A man dressed in black was locked in Lara's cage. The professor looked at the man, who just shrugged.

To Lara's amazement, the professor went over to the cage and unlocked it, helping the shadow man out. 'Good morning, Agent B,' the professor greeted him. 'Let me make you a coffee and you can tell me all about Operation Break-in.'

Now Lara was excited. This was the first time she'd seen how crafty real agents could be. The professor had set up the whole

burglary scene, just to test the reactions of the dogs. Agent B described the entire operation. He explained how PX772 had been so pathetic, allowing himself to be unlocked and then tied up. He described how ten dogs yapped in fury and how one black-and-white puppy took charge. The professor listened, open-mouthed, as he heard how Lara had escaped from her cage, rescued the disk and trapped Agent B. 'And where's the key she used?' asked the astonished professor.

Agent B coughed. 'Erm . . . well, you should get it back in a day or two, sir,' he said, opening his mouth and dropping in an imaginary key.

Professor Cortex raised his bushy eyebrows in amazement. He walked over to Lara and shook her warmly by the paw.

'GM451,' he said, 'our search is over. I would be delighted if you will do me the honour of joining me in Phase Two of the spy-dog programme. You, young lady, are our top dog.'

Lara nodded her acceptance. *Prof.*, she thought, *if you make it as exciting as last night, I'd be delighted*.

The professor had been waiting for this moment for thirty years. Phase Two training began the same day. He worked closely with GTeam, the most secretive department of a highly secret service. It was their job to devise the next generation of gadgets that could be used by animal spies.

Lara knew that a whole array of devices would be available to her, now she had been chosen as a spy dog. She had peeped in on GTeam and seen some of their ideas being developed. She had seen exploding bones, as well as hollow ones that unscrewed to hide secret papers. She knew there were collars with tracking devices. She had seen packets marked 'flea powder' that were really sleeping potions for tipping into enemy drinks. GTeam was also developing a realistic-looking dog poo that, once trodden in, would give an accurate reading of the owner's footprint. For the cats there were collars with bells – except these bells held tiny cameras, beaming pictures back to base. 'If only the cats could stay awake on their missions,' she heard the professor complain. Lara was impressed with the lizards that could change colour, camouflaging themselves in any situation. But they were too stupid to train. The professor had quite often trodden on a lizard that had blended into the floor. She knew they were developing special egg bombs for the homing pigeons, although she doubted whether the birds would ever understand how to use them. She never saw any gadgets for pigs, but she knew that a special suntan lotion was under development which would allow them to go outside for longer during the summer months. *Maybe GTeam could also develop some pig perfume to take the stink away,* she thought.

Once chosen as top dog, Lara's real training began in earnest. She was introduced to weapons and gadgets. She was fed special food and given a peak-performance fitness programme. She trained with ex-Olympic athletes and spent some time at an army training camp. She spent hours in the professor's purpose-built 'education accelerator'. This was a scary-looking machine that she was wired up to six times a day. The machine fed her information on geography, history, maths and science, allowing her to absorb vast amounts of data in a very short space of time. She slept in the learning lab and was bombarded with information, even in her sleep. Lara's brain and body grew stronger.

The professor was delighted. She had exceeded his expectations by a mile. At the age of nine months, she graduated from spy school into active service as a fully fledged spy dog.

Her most recent mission, the one which

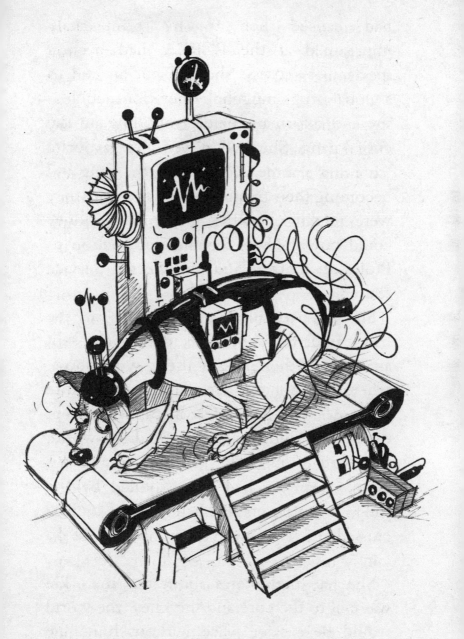

had caused her to be temporarily imprisoned at the RSPCA, had been a spectacular success. She had put an end to a global drug-smuggling operation, acting as spy and informant before rounding up the entire gang. She had played her favourite 'cute dog routine', befriending the gang and becoming their trusted pet. All the time they were feeding her the finest food money could buy, she was feeding information to Professor Cortex and the Secret Service team.

She was particularly proud of the way she had caught the gang, sunk their yacht, sent an SOS and then making them swim ashore, where the police were waiting to capture them. All were now safely in custody except the mastermind, Mr Big of the drugs world, who had escaped. He was furious that his crooked empire had been spoiled by the gang's favourite pet. He hated being double-crossed and had vowed to get his revenge on Lara.

She had nightmares about this man. He was evil to the core and she knew the world would be a safer place without him. She took particular pride in the fact that she'd managed to take some chunks out of him. In fact, it was Lara who initially caught him, sinking her teeth into his bottom and holding on until the police arrived. She could still taste his flesh — she liked the taste of baddies. But the police had let him escape. She'd gone after him and had tracked him down to a wood. He'd pulled a gun and tried to shoot her, so she'd fled, making sure she was out of his evil reach, eventually giving herself up to the RSPCA. All she had to do now was lie low with a family and await collection by the Secret Service. She was sure she wouldn't have long to wait, they

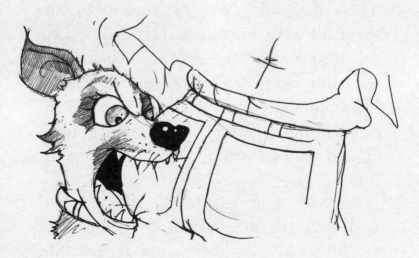

would be tracking her down right now.

She could still hear the professor's voice in her head: *'Choose a family, blend into the background, draw no attention to yourself – just be normal.'*

As the Cooks drove Lara home, they had no idea that they had chosen a spy dog. They were unaware that British Secret Service agents were systematically visiting every dog rescue shelter in the land. They had no idea that a dangerous criminal was closing in too. They thought Lara was an ordinary dog who would fit into their normal family life. Little did they suspect what lay ahead.

7. *Home Sweet Home*

Lara was a bit indignant that Dad kept calling her an 'ugly mutt', even if it was said in an affectionate way. Mum said she was 'unusual' rather than 'ugly', while the children stuck to 'cute'. Lara had never considered herself to be ugly. Intelligent, yes; ugly, no. She was about the size of a Labrador, mostly white with some big black patches on her back, tummy and face. She had one black ear that stood permanently to attention, while the other flopped helplessly over her eye. She had a black nose and black lips, a hammy pink tongue and long, spiky, black-and-white whiskers. She wiggled her bottom when she walked slowly, but she preferred to run fast. Lara consoled herself that she might be ordinary on the outside but she was very special on the inside. How many other dogs could read a map or solve jigsaw puzzles? How many were karate black belts or had GCSE Science grade A? All her fellow spy dogs could do standard doggie stuff like sniffing out drugs and biting baddies, but Lara's training had taken her well beyond that.

Her immediate problem was that she had never been treated as a normal dog. After all, attending spy school and travelling the world is hardly normal doggie behaviour. Her accelerated-learning programme was so intensive that she'd had no time to do the mundane things that most dogs take for granted. She'd never been taken for a walk. She'd been on lots of adventures and had caught dozens of criminals, but she had never been to the park and had her owner throw a stick for her to retrieve. She'd never eaten from a dog bowl, chased a cat, pooed in the garden or slept in a dog basket. Lara had been respected by everyone in the Secret Service, but never truly loved. Spy dogs didn't have time for love. But she had a vague idea of what normal dogs should do, so she decided to give it her best shot.

The Cooks arrived home and let Lara out of the car. 'Welcome to your new home, La La,' said a gleeful Ollie.

Lara cast her eye over her new, temporary home. It looked OK, a modern house with a big garden and well away from a main road. *At least I should be able to remain anonymous in a place like this*, she thought to herself.

Sophie called, 'Here, Lara. Here, girl. Come and fetch this stick,' and she threw a piece of wood down the garden.

Lara looked first at Sophie, then at Ben, and considered what to do. *She's expecting me to fetch the stick – but why, what's the point in that? She threw it, so she should fetch it herself.*

'Go on, Lara, fetch it,' Ben encouraged her.

Lara looked around. *Who? Surely not me? I definitely didn't throw it, Sophie did. I saw her do it.*

Ben became more frustrated. 'Go on, Lara, fetch the stick. Are you stupid or something?'

He's calling me stupid for not fetching a silly stick, when it wasn't even me that threw it, thought Lara, growing a bit annoyed. *OK, I'll fetch it, just this once, mind, just to prove I'm not stupid,* and she trotted off down the garden and picked the stick up in her mouth. She did a muffled bark to make sure that Ben was paying attention – and then, with a quick jerk of her head, she expertly threw the stick back to him.

Ben reached out and caught it, then looked round at his younger brother and sister, to check he hadn't imagined it.

'Cool throw,' gasped Ollie, his eyes wide in

amazement. Sophie was jumping up and down and clapping.

'Blimey, that was clever, Lara,' agreed Ben with an equally astonished look on his face. 'Most dogs bring it back rather than throwing it. Let's show Mum and Dad what you can do. Mum, come and watch Lara fetch this stick,' he enthused, tossing the stick to the other end of the garden.

Mum stood for a while, laden with tins of dog food, and watched with a smile.

'Fetch, Lara. Do what you did last time,' urged Sophie.

'Yes – go, girl,' said Ben, surprised at his own enthusiasm. 'Do your trick again.'

Lara glanced at Mum and thought for a second: *remember my orders . . . just be a normal dog.* So she obediently trotted to the other end of the garden, picked the stick up in her mouth and brought it back to Ben, dropping it neatly at his feet, just like an ordinary dog. *Sorry, kids*, thought Lara, *but I can't have grown-ups seeing my tricks, or my cover will be blown. The secret stays with us.*

'Very clever, Lara,' shouted Mum as she made one last trip from the car boot to the kitchen, carrying a bag of plastic chews and assorted doggy treats.

The children were a little disappointed. 'I wanted you to throw it back like you did last time,' whined Ben. 'Mum thinks you're just a normal dog, but we know you're special.'

For heaven's sake keep it to yourself, thought Lara, *or my secret will be out in the open and who knows what might happen then. I must be more careful*, she thought. *Blending into family life could turn out to be my most difficult mission yet!*

8. *Settling In*

Domestic life took some settling into. For a start, Lara was expected to behave like a household pet. She wasn't expected to use any of her amazing skills or talents. She took great care to conceal her superior intelligence, although the children soon suspected that Lara was something out of the ordinary.

Lara quickly grew to like the children. As the oldest, Ben was the boss. Lara knew she was officially the family pet, but she was Ben's birthday present and, in his mind, she was *his* dog. Lara loved Ben's sense of humour and the fact that he always wanted to play outdoors. She enjoyed playing football with him, although he was a bit gangly and sometimes struggled to coordinate his arms and legs. *If I'm here for any length of time, maybe we can work on those skills*, she thought. Ben had longish fair hair and his facial features fitted together as a neat package, except for his big ears, hence the long hair to conceal them. He was a bit embarrassed around girls, especially the fact that several had his name etched into their desks. His best feature was his personality – once you got to know him, that is. Ben was a shy lad, but he was the sort of person who would do anything for his mates.

Sophie was two years younger but was just as clever as Ben. She had a kind nature, reflected in a happy face with a freckle-covered nose, sparkly eyes and a cheeky giggle. Sophie adored her big brother and was like a second mum to her younger one, even if she sometimes found him really irritating. She couldn't decide whether he was annoying because he was a boy, because he was only four or because of all the pretend burps he was always doing. Perhaps it was the combination of all three that sometimes got to her.

In fact, Ollie was a carbon copy of how his

big sister had looked at four: short and stocky, with mousy hair. He considered himself a big boy now and, while Sophie would sit for hours happily drawing pictures and writing stories, he and his big brother would disappear into an imaginary world of ghosts, goblins and baddies. Which particular baddie would depend on the video he'd just watched, with most of Ollie's games involving shooting, explosions and talking in a deep baddie voice.

Mum and Dad were delighted that the children got on well together, the three of them playing nicely. Things were even better, now that Lara made four.

Lara soon became accustomed to life as a domestic pet. One of the first things that occurred to her was that dogs seemed to be treated like animals, rather than like humans. *This would certainly take some getting used to.* From day one, she decided the best plan was to observe the family and try to fit in, but she was nearly caught out on several occasions. The first night she was worn out, so she decided to go to bed early. She set the alarm clock for 4.30 a.m. so she could have an early morning fitness run, then she climbed into Mum and Dad's bed, pulled the duvet up under her chin and fell asleep.

Ben discovered her at bedtime and banished her to the dog basket. Mum and Dad were furious when the alarm went off at 4.30 the next morning.

The next day, Lara was sitting on the toilet, legs crossed, reading the newspaper (like she'd seen Dad do), when Ollie burst into the bathroom. Lara thought it a bit rude that he should come in without knocking, but she carried on in the normal way, reaching for the toilet roll and wiping her doggy bottom.

Ollie looked dumbstruck. Having only recently been toilet-trained himself, he was amazed to learn that Lara could wipe her own bottom. He still had to call Mum or Dad to help him.

Lara hadn't realized she had done anything out of the ordinary until Ollie piped up at teatime, 'Lara sat on the toilet to do her poo and I helped flush it because it was a big one.' The talk of poo and toilets caused Dad to put his knife and fork down, temporarily losing his appetite.

'Of course, Ollie,' said Mum, not taking a blind bit of notice, thinking that he was in one of his fantasy worlds again. 'She'll be sitting at the table, eating her dinner, next!'

The following day, Sophie caught Lara doing exactly that. Mum had gone to round up the family for tea, and Sophie arrived in the kitchen to find Lara sitting at the table, napkin tucked into her collar, waiting for her meal. Lara wagged her tail enthusiastically and sipped her orange juice through a straw. 'Bad dog, Lara.' Sophie frowned.

Lara looked puzzled. *Oh dear, what have I done now?*

'Dogs don't sit at the table or eat carrots and broccoli,' explained Sophie in a stern voice, wagging her finger like Mum sometimes did. 'And they certainly don't drink orange squash, especially not through a straw.'

Lara raised an eyebrow in surprise. *Don't we indeed? What exactly do we do? she wondered.*

Sophie continued the lecture. 'They eat dog food out of a bowl, on the floor. And they slurp water with their tongue, not through a straw.'

Dog food . . . bowl . . . floor . . . thanks for the warning, she thought, quickly climbing down from her chair and trying to look innocent, just as Mum and Dad came into the kitchen to sit down for tea. *That was a close shave. I must try and behave more like an ordinary dog.*

She snuggled down into her dog basket, looking solemn-faced and slightly stupid, with one ear up, one ear down and the napkin still tucked into her collar. *The sooner I'm rescued the better!*

9. The Chase is On

Professor Cortex grew more and more anxious by the day. 'We must double our efforts!' he shouted at his morning meeting. His fist hit the table so hard, teacups jumped out of their saucers and his people automatically reached for hankies to wipe up the mess. The professor appeared not to notice. He looked at the team assembled round the table and glared at each and every one. These were the finest agents in the British Secret Service, yet they couldn't find his dog. He smoothed his three strands of hair back across his head and regained his composure. 'GM451 is my life's work,' he explained, a little more calmly. 'There will be trouble for us all if she falls into the wrong hands. Do you get my meaning?'

There were collective nods round the table. 'Yes, sir, Professor,' said the Secret Service team leader. 'Leave it to us, sir. We will find GM451 and get her back here pronto, sir.' The room cleared as the team of spies left to continue their search.

Professor Cortex was left alone. He drummed his fingers on the table and pursed his lips as he considered the situation. He was certain that enemy agents would be looking for his spy dog. He was equally certain that Mr Big of the drug world would be searching for GM451. After all, it was she who had rounded up his entire gang, and this particularly evil man would stop at nothing to get his revenge. The professor muttered aloud to himself, 'He's a nasty piece of work. We had better find you soon, GM451, or things could turn very ugly indeed.' Professor Cortex knew he was in a race, one in which there would be no prizes for coming second.

'I chose him from the dog shelter and I've called him Alfie,' explained the football-shirted fat man to the stranger in the pub.

'He's a good dog . . . well, apart from biting the postman, that is.' The fat man bent down and scratched behind Alfie's ear. 'He's a fine-looking hound, though, don't you reckon?

Mr Big looked at Alfie's cauliflower face and thought him the ugliest dog he'd ever seen. *And why do dogs always look like their owners?* he wondered as Alfie slouched in a heap, rolls of fat spilling over his collar.

'Yes, he's quite a looker,' lied the drug-dealer. 'But tell me more about the black-and-white one you nearly chose.'

The fat man rummaged in his ear. 'Like I was saying, I nearly chose this black-and-white dog, but it had funny ears and I'm not sure it was house-trained. Might have had fleas too. I hate dirty, disgusting animals,' he said.

'Quite,' mused Mr Big, who hadn't said much but had listened very carefully, especially when the large man had mentioned a dog with odd ears. 'The black-and-white one sounds perfect for me,' he said. 'What exactly did it look like?'

The fat man pulled his little finger out of his ear and admired the amount of wax. 'Well,' he said, wiping his finger on his shirt,

'it was kind of funny-looking. One ear up and one ear down. A bit ugly, actually. Not like my Alfie.'

Mr Big stroked his goatee beard. 'So, if I went to the same place as you did, I could get the black-and-white one? I always feel sorry for the dogs that aren't chosen,' he lied. 'Which dog shelter did you say it was?'

The large man took a swig of gassy beer and belched, wiping his sleeve across his mouth. 'The local one,' he said helpfully, pointing to the pub door. 'Turn right and then left at the supermarket. The RSPCA is about a hundred metres down that road.'

The stranger took a fake fifty-pound note from his wallet and handed it to the football-shirted man. 'Thank you, my friend,' he muttered. 'Buy yourself a new shirt, and get a little something for Alfie.' He smirked then drained the rest of his beer.

'Thanks very much, mate,' beamed the fat man. 'You are a very nice chap indeed,' he added. He had always been a poor judge of character.

Mr Big left the pub and turned right towards the RSPCA.

10. *A Dog's Worst Friend*

Mr Big, Lara's number-one enemy, entered the local RSPCA. Without looking up from her paperwork the receptionist said, 'Please take a seat and I'll be with you in a minute.'

The man tenderly touched the bite wounds on his bottom, wincing as he felt the deep teeth marks. 'I'd rather stand,' he said briskly. He looked around at the dozens of thank-you letters and the pictures of happy dogs with their loving families, and he felt sick to the pit of his stomach. He hated dogs, loathed them with a passion. The lady looked busy and he wasn't one for wasting time, so he approached the desk purposefully and asked her if there had been any black-and-white dogs taken away in the last few days.

The lady laughed out loud. 'Hundreds of them, my dear man,' she explained, again without looking up from her paperwork.

'With one ear up and one ear down?' quizzed the man.

It was such a strange description, the woman looked up at last. She saw a tall man in a black leather coat and a smart designer suit, sporting a goatee beard and narrow black sideburns. His dark eyes looked straight into hers, making her feel uneasy.

'One ear up and one down, black and white,' he repeated slowly and menacingly.

The lady was worried by his tone but tried to remain calm. 'Hundreds of them,' she repeated carefully. 'Why do you want to know?'

'It was my dog,' blurted the man unconvincingly. 'And I want her back because I love her so.'

This man's never had a dog in his life, thought the woman. She didn't think he was capable of love – he was too cold and menacing.

'Look, lady, I really love this dog and I must have her back, like now,' he said impatiently.

'Lots of dogs pass through this place, I can't remember any one in particular.'

'I advise you to remember this one,' said the man icily.

The receptionist shivered. She noticed scratch marks on the backs of his hands. She was becoming more concerned. She knew of only one black-and-white dog with odd ears, a dog that a fat, football-shirted man said had given him fleas. That dog had left several days ago and had gone to a nice home with three children, but she wasn't going to tell this thug, that was for sure.

'We have lots of dogs, why not choose yourself another one?' said the lady, going along with his story and smiling weakly.

Mr Big was desperate to get his hands on the dog but knew he had to remain calm. 'I don't think you understand,' he smiled through gritted teeth. 'I have to have *this* one. If you don't help me, I will have to take the law into my own hands. I have to find this dog, she's valuable to me.' The woman clearly wasn't going to talk, so he changed tactics. 'OK, lady, let me go and take a look,' he said, his eyes settling on a large bunch of keys on the counter. 'You're right, maybe I should choose another.' He left the office and walked out into the yard, slipping the keys into his pocket as he went.

Once in the yard, he began to unlock the cages, releasing half a dozen of the smaller dogs. They could sense that he was evil and began to snap at his ankles, ripping his trousers in the process. 'Shoo, you horrible creatures,' he yelled, kicking them away.

Mr Big banged on the office window and the lady looked out, horrified to see the dogs attacking a customer. She raced out and grabbed as many dogs as she could.

'Oh, I'm so sorry, I don't know how they got out. Are you OK, sir?' she flustered.

'Just get these blasted dogs off me,' he shouted, kicking out once more as the dogs yapped around him.

As the lady struggled to control the mayhem he calmly walked back into the office and, jumping over the counter, began to rummage through the drawers and filing cabinets. It didn't take him long to find the customer address book, and he put it in his inside jacket pocket. He hurdled the counter once more and left, slamming the door behind him.

Mr Big marched away purposefully. He would visit each of the owners until he found the dog that had betrayed him. Behind him, fifty-six RSPCA dogs were howling in fury. They could smell danger and they knew he was a bad man. He was ahead in the race to find Lara. The only problem was, if he found her first, she would be in big trouble.

11. *Bully Boys*

Ollie already knew. Sophie suspected early on, and Ben took a little longer to be totally convinced that Lara was special, but the penny dropped when the three of them took her for a walk in the park. Lara had never been for a walk – well, not a walk for walk's sake. She'd done assault courses and endurance runs and had tracked criminals for hundreds of kilometres, but she had never been on a walk for fun. *What's the point?* she asked herself when the children told her they were taking her for 'walkies'. Ben clipped a lead to Lara's collar and waited impatiently while Ollie put his socks on. 'Come on, slowcoach,' he urged as his younger brother finally pulled on his wellies, albeit on the wrong feet.

'We're taking Lara for a walk,' Ollie told Mum.

'Make sure she stays on the lead, otherwise she may run off,' warned Mum. 'And look after her because she may be scared of other dogs.'

I beg your pardon, madam, thought Lara. *Scared of other dogs? I'm a trained fighter, if you please. Other dogs are more likely to be scared of me!*

The children set off, skipping along excitedly, with Lara trotting beside them, slightly confused by the whole experience. *I still don't get the point. We're too slow for it to be a keep-fit exercise, and we don't seem to be going anywhere in particular, so why are we going for a walk?*

In a couple of minutes they arrived at the park. It was still fairly early so they had the place more or less to themselves. 'Look, Lara, we've brought you a special ball all of your own,' chirped an excited Sophie, producing a blue rubber ball from her coat pocket.

Great, wow, I can hardly contain my excitement – not! What do I want with a ball? Who do they think I am, a Premiership footballer?

Sophie unclipped Lara's lead and handed the ball to Ben, who hurled it as far as he could. 'Fetch your new ball, Lara,' he encouraged.

I suppose I ought to show willing. After all, I'm supposed to be acting like a normal household pet, thought Lara, and she bounded off to find the ball. She soon sniffed it out. Remembering to pick it up in her mouth rather than her paws, she returned it to her new owner. Ben was clearly delighted and fussed around Lara as if she had just found the Crown Jewels. *Steady, lad, it's only a ball*, thought Lara, beginning to warm to the children's enthusiasm. Seeing the youngsters' faces light up was very satisfying. Lara realized that she was bringing pleasure to all three and that she was actually enjoying playing with them.

Sophie tossed the ball a second, third and fourth time. Lara's enthusiasm increased each time, and the children were thrilled to see their dog enjoy herself. It was on the fifth throw that they realized Lara was special. This time Ben hurled the ball as far as he could, and it rolled down a grassy bank, coming to rest in some long grass at the bottom. Lara bounded off dutifully to retrieve the ball, *her* ball. She was just about to turn and race back to the children when two huge black-and-brown dogs sprang out of the long grass. They were Rottweilers, bred to look fierce, designed to bark and bite. This pair of dogs looked particularly scary, all muscle, curled lips, sharp teeth and studded collars. Even worse was their snarling attitude. Who are you? growled Rottweiler number one. This is our park and we don't like new dogs coming on to our patch.

Boys, boys, boys, woofed Lara reassuringly. *Is this any way to treat a visitor? I'm here with my new owners, just to have a bit of fun, so stop snarling and leave me alone. Besides, you've no idea who or what you're dealing with, so stand aside and stop curling your lips like that, it's so ugly. Treat this as a friendly warning: stand aside or you'll be sorry.*

The two muscle-bound dogs looked at each other in a slightly puzzled manner. This wasn't the kind of answer they were used to. Then the larger of the dogs burst into deep canine laughter. How dare this sticky-up-eared mongrel answer them back? Nobody did that and got away with it. *We'll be sorry, will we? I don't think so, darlin'. Spike and me is the toughest dogs in this neighbourhood and nobody messes with us.*

Well, boys, sorry to burst your bubble, but I think you are now second and third hardest dogs in the neighbourhood – after me! growled Lara, full of confidence. She knew Rottweilers were pretty tough animals, but she was confident that her training would come in handy if they were keen for a fight. Lara was used to being top dog and wasn't going to be pushed around by a couple of bullies. Although they towered over her, she could easily outsmart this pair – and she could kick their butts too if need be.

I think she needs to be taught a lesson. What do you reckon, Fang? asked Spike.

Fang twitched with excitement, just as he always did before a big fight – not that he was expecting this puny girl dog to be much of a match for him and his brother. *Yeah, let's sort her out and then frighten the life out of those kids. I think that'd be a lesson worth learning, don't you?*

At this point the children came galloping down the hill, looking for their dog, and saw the two Rottweilers growling at Lara, as if warning her off. Ben was about to call Lara to him to get her back on the lead when the Rottweilers attacked.

Fang and Spike had obviously bullied dogs before and they leapt in team formation, knocking Lara off her feet.

She quickly righted herself and assessed the situation. *Stay calm and think. Remember your training.* Hackles raised, she gave a low growl, *I've warned you, boys, back off or else.* She had no choice. She was in peril from these two meatheads — but, more importantly, the children were now also at risk. Special action was needed.

The Rottweilers rounded on her again, this time one from the front and one from the side in a fierce pincer movement. Lara surprised them by rising to stand

on her hind legs, adopting a low, crouching judo stance. Ollie had seen this in a *Karate Kid* film and explained to an open-mouthed Ben that Lara must be a karate-dog.

As Spike attacked from the front, Lara karate chopped

him on the head, knocking him to the ground, while at the same time sticking out her left leg and tripping the oncoming Fang, sending both dogs, nose first, into the mud. Lara circled on her hind legs, still in karate style, shadow boxing as she danced round the flattened Rottweilers. *Come on then, boys. Get up. You can't teach me a lesson while you lounge about like that*, she teased, delighted that her training was being put to good use.

'Lara, we'd better go quick,' said Sophie, 'before those horrible dogs decide to attack again.'

Too late. Fang, whose pride had been hurt more than his backside, leapt at Lara, this time with a look in his eyes that made Sophie squeal with terror.

She needn't have worried. Once again Lara floored the flying bully with a karate chop. Fang crashed to the ground like a felled boxer, out for the count and unable to do the children any harm. His two front teeth lay next to him, glistening white against the green grass. Spike thought better of trying to fight Lara and slunk away, quite unable to believe that he'd just witnessed a girl dog duff up his brother.

Sophie called Lara again, this time with more urgency. As she clipped the lead on to Lara's collar Sophie said, 'That was very clever and very brave. How did you know karate? Dogs can't do karate, or whistle or eat broccoli . . . or drink through a straw.'

'Or use a toilet,' piped up Ollie.

'Or throw sticks,' added Ben. 'We don't think you're a very normal dog.'

That's for sure. I don't mind the three of you knowing, but the secret must stay with us, thought Lara as she obediently trotted home. *If grown-ups find out that I'm a highly trained spy dog, then I'm in trouble.*

From then on Lara was supremely careful about how she behaved. She figured that the kids already knew she was special, so there was no use hiding it from them. Her objective must be to hide her secret from the adults. *After all,* she thought, *it can't be too long before my Secret Service owners find me and all will be back to normal.*

12. *All in a Day's Work*

Lara had learnt the basics of domestic life and had settled in remarkably well, almost to the point where she was enjoying being showered with affection and belonging to a family. She thought back to her spying days; sure, they were good times and she had been admired and respected, but never truly loved – at least not in the way Ben, Sophie and Ollie loved her. Lara had found contentment and happiness. Her spy-dog duties had been exciting, but every day she missed them less and less. Her duties as a family pet seemed to be more worthwhile. The Secret Service could probably get a new spy dog, but the Cooks couldn't get another Lara.

On weekdays the family went their separate ways: Mum and Dad to work, Ollie to nursery and the older children to school. Lara was expected to stay at Gran's, across the road, although the reality was that she was allowed to roam fairly freely. Ollie gave Gran special orders on Lara's first day. 'If she whistles or anything, just ignore her. And don't upset her, otherwise she might do karate-dog on you, just like she did to those horrible dogs in the park.'

'Goodness me. It sounds as if I'd better treat Lara very well indeed, otherwise she'll be roughing me up,' chuckled Gran, making a mental note not to feed her grandson so many E-numbers, as they were clearly affecting his imagination.

Ben gave his dog a huge hug before sadly trudging off to school. 'See you for a kick-about later,' he shouted. Of all the family, Ben had bonded with the new dog the most and they had become best pals, even though they'd only had Lara for a few days.

Gran fussed around Lara, giving her custard creams and even letting her lick the spilt tea out of her saucer. Despite the old lady's kindness, Lara soon got bored. There was simply nothing to do except watch

daytime TV or read the newspaper. Lara was interested to see that interest rates had gone up and the value of the dollar had fallen against the euro. While Gran busied herself in the pantry, Lara carefully finished off the newspaper crossword. *Fancy the old dear not knowing the capital of Mongolia!* Local news said that a huge shipment of drugs had been smuggled into the region and that the police were searching for the gang responsible. *The usual stuff*, thought Lara and, as Gran nodded off, she decided to investigate the neighbourhood to see whether anything interesting was going on. After all, she considered, it would be a waste of her training to sit curled up by the fire all day. She was beginning to enjoy her extended holiday from the Secret Service.

Lara jumped up on her hind legs and let herself out of the house. Gran snored on, oblivious.

The Cooks lived in a nice part of town, nestled on the outskirts, surrounded by parks and woodland. Lara navigated the local area with ease, taking care when crossing roads. She sniffed her way around the local shops without finding anything of particular interest. She spied a young man shoplifting in the local grocery store and growled menacingly enough for him to hastily return the cans of lager to the shelf.

Lara ambled through the local park, keeping an eye out for Fang and Spike. Rottweilers with wounded pride could be very dangerous indeed, if a little stupid into the bargain. *No sign of them. They must be still licking their wounds*. In the distance a woman was walking her dog. Lara smiled with pride as the dog bounced up and down in the way that only Bruce could. *Now there's a happy ending.*

To investigate further, Lara left the park and sniffed her way to the industrial end of town. This was more grimy and noisy, with some very interesting smells: petrol, sewers, rats and the satisfying smell of bacon and sausage from Alf's 'All Day Breakfast' Cafe. Suddenly she caught a whiff of something very familiar, something she'd been trained to sniff out at airports. *Surely not. It can't be. Not here in the middle of town?*

She sniffed again, nose in the air, concentration on her face. No mistaking it this time, Lara could pick out the smell of drugs. They mingled with the other smells of the industrial estate, but there were definitely drugs in there somewhere. *Which direction was the smell coming from? Sniff again and think.* A van whizzed by and the aroma of drugs was lost temporarily in a cloud of exhaust fumes. Lara shook her head to clear her airways, her ears flapping wildly. *Start again, concentrate hard and remember your training.*

Nose to the ground, she soon picked up the trail, faint at first but gradually getting stronger. Her nose led her to a warehouse. It seemed a little run-down, with smashed windows and peeling paint. The sign at the front gate proclaimed 'Harry's High Quality Meat', but Lara couldn't imagine there being anything 'quality' about this place. There was a white van parked in the car park and a lorry round the back, but no sign of Harry, his staff or any customers.

The strong smell of drugs tempted Lara to investigate further. She was trained to stop drug runners from entering the country, but if one had slipped through the net then she might as well sort it out here and now. *I can't turn a blind eye to crime.* A plan began to form in her mind.

Lara stood on her hind legs and stretched to peer through one of the grubby windows. She spat on her paw and rubbed the glass to see more clearly, and she could just make out a small group of men unloading a lorry at the back of the warehouse. Apart from that, the place was almost empty except for some workbenches and huge fridges that Harry obviously used to store his meat. The door was bolted on the inside. She would have to play the dumb dog routine to get in, so she squeezed under a gate and padded her way innocently to the back door. Here she saw the lorry, its front end poking out of the building, its rear end reversed into the loading bay, its engine still running. The smell of drugs was now so strong that it drowned out the fumes belching from the lorry's exhaust pipe.

Lara sat and thought through her plan. One of the men came out of the warehouse and jumped up into the lorry cab to fetch his cigarettes and mobile phone. He glanced at Lara. 'Shoo, mutt. Harry's gone so there's no meat for ya, no bones, no nothing – except this boot up yer backside,' he said, standing on one leg for a moment and pointing to his right shoe.

Charming, thought Lara as she sat and wagged her tail at him, trying her very best to look like a normal dog. *Obviously not an animal lover, and probably a drug dealer too, not a nice combination.*

She waited until the coast was clear and

then put the first piece of her plan into action. She approached the idling lorry and reached for the fuel cap. With some difficulty she managed to unscrew it and place it carefully by her feet. Next she went to a nearby hose and picked it up in her teeth. She put the end of the hose into the fuel tank and went to turn on the tap. Water flowed into the petrol tank of the lorry, filling it to the top. Lara turned the tap off and returned the hose to its place, before screwing the fuel cap back on. Phew, job done, she thought. Now for the second part of the plan.

Lara sneaked into the warehouse and watched the men unloading the lorry. They were stacking large bags of white powder in one corner of the warehouse. Lara wasn't sure what kind of drugs they were, but she knew that if these dealers sold them they would cause great harm to people and, from the look of it, this was a large haul.

She thought about whether to run for help. *The police perhaps, if I can find anyone? What about a member of the public? No, they would just think I was a barking mad dog and wouldn't understand what I was on about. No, I will have to sort this one out myself.*

Lara confidently walked out of her hiding place, in full view of the drug dealers unloading the wagon.

'There's that ugly mutt again,' said the man to his fellow criminals. 'I told her that if I saw her again she'd get some of this,' he said, pointing to his boot again.

'It's only a stupid dog. Stop stressin',' said his mate, 'and get on with unloadin' the gear. Raymond'll be 'ere in ten minutes with the cash, so we'd better be finished or he'll turn nasty on us.'

Ah, thought Lara, *Raymond must be coming here too, that's handy. I'll try and get them all put in jail at the same time.*

Lara sat and watched the men as they worked feverishly to unload bag after bag of white powder from the lorry. The men ignored the black-and-white dog. They were too busy to bother, although the animal-hater kept swearing at her and growling in her direction. 'I'll set my dogs on ya one day, you 'orrible 'ound,' he snarled. 'Spike and Fang'll sort yer out all right, just as soon as

Fang's broken jaw's mended.'

Spike and Fang are stupid bullies, thought Lara, *but now it makes sense. Horrible man owns horrible dogs. It's no wonder that Fang and Spike are so aggressive if that's how they've been brought up!*

The men completed their task, stacking the bags in a neat pile, just in time to see a smart new motor car pull up at the back gates. 'Must be Raymond and his boys,' said one of the men. 'Chill out, lads, it's cash time,' he smiled, rubbing his hands in glee.

I don't think so, thought Lara, *at least not if my plan comes off.* She calmly wandered over to the pile of white drug-filled bags and started dragging one over towards Harry's giant fridges that stood with its door wedged open.

At first nobody noticed, then Raymond entered the warehouse, stood stock-still and bellowed, 'What's that dog doin' with my merchandise?' The whole gang looked round, to see Lara disappearing into the warehouse freezer, dragging a bag in her jaws. It was heavy going but, once inside the huge cooler, Lara hid the bag behind a workbench. The next part of the plan was much easier than she'd ever imagined. As soon as they saw what Lara was doing, the gang of men, Raymond and his heavies included, ran full speed into the giant fridge. Lara dodged between legs and away from grasping hands, tripping up as many men as she could. She slipped out in the confusion, removed the doorstop and watched the heavy iron door swing shut. She quickly stood on her hind legs and snapped the bolt into place.

She stood upright and peered into the freezer through a little glass window, pleased by what she saw. The gang had found the bag of drugs but couldn't get out. Lara waved at them. They were clearly not happy, banging and kicking on the door in a vain attempt to break it down, but Harry's fridges were in much better shape than the rest of his warehouse. The men were trapped and completely helpless.

I hope they've remembered their coats, thought Lara wistfully, turning the thermostat to 'maximum chill'.

The final part of her plan was to get help. She heard a noise and turned – to see the

animal-hater guarding the exit. He was carrying a large spanner, slapping it menacingly into the palm of his hand. 'Me versus you then, pooch,' he growled.

Lara was worried. *He really does look scary,* she thought. *But hopefully he's as stupid and cowardly as Fang and Spike.* She growled a warning, and the man hesitated. Gaining in confidence, she growled her fiercest growl, hackles raised, showing that she meant business. The man took a step back, looking round to see where the exit was. Lara stalked forward, slowly, one foot at a time, a low growl in her throat. The man took several steps backwards. Lara sprang, and he dropped the spanner and fled.

He jumped into the lorry and locked the door. Hands shaking, he turned the key, and the engine spluttered and died. He punched the steering wheel in frustration and tried again. Same result. *Poor man*, barked Lara. *Someone's tampered with your lorry.*

Lara sprinted out of the warehouse into the street. Bruce and his owner were just passing. Bruce was delighted to see Lara and immediately started bouncing again. *Hi, Lara*, he barked. *How fantastic it is to see you. I hope you found as good a home as I have?*

Lara considered for a moment. *You know what, Bruce, I have. It's absolutely brilliant. Better than I could ever have imagined. But I can't stop and chat. You know you said you owe me a favour? Can I call it in right now?*

For you, anything, he barked. *What do you want me to do?*

Lara barked quick orders. Bruce was rather surprised, but it was the least he could do. At last being big and gruff was an advantage. He held his head high and stood guard outside the lorry while Lara went for help. Bruce's owner pulled and tugged at his lead, but Bruce stood firm, proudly guarding the animal-hater.

Lara raced back home very quickly, her speed and fitness training being put to good effect. Without hesitation she jumped up on to the dustbin, then on to the low garage roof of the Cooks' house and wriggled in through the bathroom window. Once inside, she went to Dad's study and switched on the computer. It took ages to boot up. Lara entered a new password she had recently set up and opened her email account. Typing is difficult for a dog, what with having clumsy paws instead of hands, so she found it quicker and easier to tap out the words using a pencil held in her mouth. She rushed the typing, so it wasn't perfect; but when she thought about it, it wasn't bad for a dog.

deer policE. There R some dRug dealers locked in a giant FRidge at Harrys Quality Meat WarEHouse on Station ROAd. There R 46 sacks of Drugs on the premISes and a dog called Bruce gArding the eEExit. Pleas3 hurry or Bruces owner will LOSe patience and he will b in tGrouble. Please bring blankets 4 tHe men will b very cold
Tha4NKs.

There was nothing more to be done. Lara clicked the 'send' button, logged off the computer, went out through the bathroom window and let herself back into Gran's house.

Lara curled up by the fire and shut her eyes for a bit of a snooze, only to be awoken by the snorting of Gran waking up. 'Ooh, must have dozed off,' croaked the old lady.

Too right, thought Lara. *For four and a half hours, to be exact!*

'Still curled up by the fire, eh?' She smiled to Lara. 'You lazy pup. A young thing like you should be out and about, getting into mischief, not wasting your day sitting by the fire doing nothing.'

Before Lara had time to be indignant, the local TV news came on.

'The main news today,' declared the presenter. 'Drug dealers in the cooler, caught by local police after a tip-off; shoplifter caught returning goods to the store; plus local weather and sport.' Gran listened on and off while Lara concentrated hard, hanging on every word. 'Police have today seized the biggest haul of cocaine for twenty-five years, catching the gang red-handed. Raymond Coleman, a wanted criminal long suspected of drug offences, has finally been arrested at the scene of the crime in what police are claiming to be their most important breakthrough in recent times. The men had become trapped inside an industrial cooler, with their vehicle sabotaged in what the chief inspector has called an elaborate and clever plan. Drug-squad officers acted on an email tip-off, finding the gang securely imprisoned, while a local dog stood guard outside.' Next came some footage of the gang being led away, teeth chattering. The chief inspector was then interviewed, smiling broadly, no doubt thinking about his certain promotion. He spoke of now giving these criminals time to cool off in prison. 'They're in custody right now,' he declared proudly, 'sipping hot chocolate.'

Very clever, thought Lara with a huge grin on her doggy face. *Nice one, Chief Inspector, trapped in a fridge and 'cooling off in prison' – very funny indeed.*

'There you go,' said Gran, picking up half the story. 'While we have a little nap, that dog – What was his name? Bruce? – was battling against evil drug barons. The adventures some people have! And to think we snoozed all afternoon.' She chuckled to herself and Lara.

Snoozed all afternoon, thought Lara. *You might have done, but I consider it a day well spent.*

Lara's keen ears picked up the sound of footsteps rattling up the garden path, moments before the door was flung almost off its hinges and the children burst into Gran's kitchen.

'Lara!' shouted Ben warmly, throwing his arms round his pet's neck and ignoring his grandmother completely. 'We've missed you. I hope you've been a good girl. I hope Gran's been looking after you?'

'She's been no trouble, kids,' announced Gran. 'In fact, she'll probably need a walk, because she's been curled up by the fire for most of the afternoon.'

Ben reached for her ball. 'I'll just get changed, and then we can go for a play outside. What do you reckon, girl?'

Lara wagged her tail furiously, like normal dogs do. She was doing a lot of that lately. She thought about her day with a warm glow in her inside that showed as a silly doggy grin on the outside. *Family life is fantastic.*

13. *Danger Lurks*

Not many miles away, a man sporting a goatee beard and a sore bottom was also watching the news. His designer suit was ripped round the ankles. He was weary from trudging around the houses, checking up on RSPCA dogs. Lesser men would have given up, but not him; he was driven by revenge, entirely focused on finding the black-and-white spy dog that had ruined his life.

He sat in a dingy hotel room and flicked on the TV. As the picture sparked into life, he stretched out his right arm and looked at the scars that ran its length. They were now itchy and scabbed over, but he was sure they would leave a permanent reminder of *that* dog – the animal that had put paid to his entire crooked operation. The dog that he would soon find and destroy – not today, maybe, but very soon. He had followed up 187 of the names on the RSPCA list of 211; he would soon hit the jackpot. He smiled at his evil thoughts. He would eliminate the dog forever – and the family too, if they got in his way.

The local news caught his attention. A big drugs bust linked with a dog – could it be that the spy dog was involved? He listened carefully. The dog was called Bruce and the TV pictures clearly showed it to be brown and white, so forget it, it couldn't be. The one he was looking for was black and white with a sticky-up ear. Then Bruce's proud owner came on, interviewed by the reporter. 'Of course Bruce was a hero,' she agreed enthusiastically. 'He kept guard while the drug gang was trapped inside. He's my little hero, aren't you, Brucey?' she proclaimed as she stroked his muzzle. 'Of course, I think that other dog helped a bit, that black-and-white one with a sticky-up ear who ran off. I think she told you there were some baddies inside, but you were the brave little soldier who stood guard.'

The man sat bolt upright. 'Black-and-white one,' he growled out loud. 'Sticky-up ear. I think we're getting warmer.' He tapped the number of the local TV station into his mobile phone. He intended to get the full story and hunt down the black-and-white dog.

14. *A Near Miss*

Professor Cortex couldn't control his anger and frustration any longer. 'He did what?' bellowed the normally mild-mannered scientist, showering the special agent in spit.

The head of the Secret Service reached for a hanky to mop his face, and he tried to remain calm. 'We can't be sure it was him, Professor, but it certainly matches his description. He entered the RSPCA late yesterday afternoon and caused a lot of confusion. The lady says it took her a while to get the dogs back in the cages.'

'And . . . and . . .' demanded the professor, turning purple.

'And, sir, it wasn't until this morning that she noticed that the customer address book was missing. Seems like our friend may have snatched it in the confusion,' winced the spy master.

'Snatched it in the confusion!' exploded the professor, showering the man again. 'So Mr Big has the complete list of all the owners of all the adopted dogs. And what do we have? Tell me, Agent A, what has your expert team come up with?'

The man looked down at his highly polished shoes. 'Er, nothing, sir,' he admitted.

'Nothing indeed,' agreed Professor Cortex. 'A big fat zero.'

Agent A perked up a little. 'Except the RSPCA lady says she does remember a dog fitting the description of GM451.' He flicked through his notebook. 'Apparently the dog was chosen by a family with three kids. The lady says that one of the kids said the dog could whistle. She obviously thought it was a joke, sir.'

Professor Cortex wasn't smiling.

'We do have an address, Professor. Would you like us to pay a visit?'

Professor Cortex was beyond anger. 'That would be very good of you, Agent A,' he replied calmly. 'And if you don't find her, you can start thinking about a career lower down the alphabet!' he bellowed as the chief spy turned and hurried out.

The professor was alone. He sank into his office chair, sucking in lungfuls of air. 'Be calm, Maximus,' he soothed himself aloud. 'Remember what the doctor said about your blood pressure.' He reached into his desk drawer and took out a box of pills, his hands shaking with frustration. The professor rattled three coloured pills into the palm of his hand and scoffed them in one go. He pulled a face and reached for a glass of water. Gradually the tension eased and he allowed himself to relax in his chair.

He couldn't believe that his expert team had been outwitted by Mr Big. They could no longer be trusted. The professor pressed a button on his phone. 'Agent A, pick me up at the main entrance. I'm coming along for the ride.'

The Cooks had been looking forward to their holiday for months, and at last the day had arrived. Of course, when they'd booked it there was no mention of a dog, so Dad had phoned the landlady to check that Lara could come too. The plan of leaving her with Gran had backfired. Ben had laid down an ultimatum: if Lara had to stay, he would too. 'Lara's part of the family, Dad,' he argued, 'so she has to come to the seaside with us – end of story.' In fact, it was less of an argument and more a statement of intent, so Mum and Dad relented, knowing how much Lara meant to the children.

So Lara was coming too and, although she hated to admit it, she was rather looking forward to a family beach holiday. For the moment, the sun was shining and everyone was in an excited mood as Lara leapt into the back of the car and they set off.

As they disappeared round the corner, Mr Big approached from the other direction, pulling his car up outside the Cooks' locked-up house. He surveyed the situation carefully, before reaching into his glove compartment and pulling out a pair of leather gloves that fitted his scratched hands snugly. Then out of the glove compartment came a revolver, complete with silencer. He

tucked the weapon into his jacket pocket. There was no point in frightening the neighbours, he decided. He was thoughtful like that.

Mr Big opened the front gate, sneering at the 'Beware of the Dog' sign. 'Poxy mutt had better beware of me and my shooter, more like,' he growled under his breath. He knocked loudly on the front door. No answer. He was just about to go round the back when Gran appeared from across the road.

'They've gone away for a couple of days, dear,' she told him. 'Down to Devon, I think, to make the most of this glorious weather. It is lovely, isn't it?'

'How long?' grunted the man.

'The weatherman says about two weeks.'

'Not the weather, lady. How long have they gone for and where to exactly?' he shouted impatiently. He decided he could just as well visit them in their hotel. A dead dog's a dead dog, wherever he killed her.

'Just three nights. North Devon, I think, or was it south?'

'Did they leave an address?'

'No, dear, but I'll let them know you called. What's your name again, I don't think I caught it?'

'Doesn't matter,' he growled. 'I'll be here when they get back, you can be sure of that.'

'OK, dear,' said Gran, smiling. *What a jolly nice fellow*, she thought to herself as she closed the door on the villain.

One hour later, Gran noticed another visitor across the road. Her net curtains twitched as she took a closer look – it wasn't just one person, it was a whole vanload of men, all dressed in black suits and shades. She counted them: six of the dark-glasses variety, plus one bald-headed old man – well, bald

except for three hairs combed across his head. Gran watched as the men circled the Cooks' house, talking to each other on radios. As one of the young men jumped over the Cooks' garden wall, she saw with horror that he had a gun tucked inside his jacket. The old lady froze with fear. She could overhear them shouting to one another. It sounded like, 'Yes, Professor, looks like this could be the one. I'll wait here and get them when they return.'

'Oh my great goodness,' gasped Gran. 'The man with the gun says he's going to get them when they return!' The terrified old lady reached for the telephone and dialled 999.

15. *Family Fun*

The Cooks were thoroughly enjoying their holiday. The sun shone every day and they all ate far too many cream teas and ice creams. Mum and Dad sat, smiling, as the children and Lara dug holes in the sand and went crabbing and paddling together.

'She's a fantastic mutt – not very pretty, but really fantastic,' said Mum, out of earshot of the kids as they dug yet another hole in the golden sand.

'Sure is,' agreed Dad. 'I can't believe how quickly she's become part of the family and how much the kids love her.'

It may have been out of the children's earshot, but not out of Lara's, and she dug faster and deeper, almost exploding with pride. She had changed her view on life.

Sure, the Secret Service stuff was exciting, but this was where she really belonged. Rather than looking forward to the day her handlers turned up to claim her, she was dreading it. How could she leave Ben, Sophie and Ollie? They would be distraught and, thinking about it, she would be too. She would miss them terribly. *Still, it might not happen*, she thought. *It's been four weeks since I gave myself up to the RSPCA and there's no sign of rescue yet. Maybe they've tried to find me and failed. Maybe they've given up looking. Maybe they think I'm dead. Maybe I'm not as valuable as I thought and they've decided I'm not worth the effort and money to track down.* She hoped, truly hoped, that they had given up and she could spend the rest of her life in doggie heaven, which, to her, was being part of a loving family and having fun with Ben, Sophie and Ollie.

Lara had hardly needed to use her special skills at all. In fact, only once during the entire holiday. There were some German tourists who were lost, chattering among themselves in German about the best way to get to Croyde. While Mum and Dad walked on, oblivious to the German language, Lara hung back and winked at Ben. She joined the tourists at their picnic table and studied their map. She stabbed her paw at Croyde village, then leapt to her feet and pointed the way, jabbing her paw towards the next headland. The tourists were astonished. Not only could this dog read a map and give directions, it could also understand German! Ben just laughed, not a bit surprised. He and Lara had an understanding. Ben knew that Lara couldn't talk – well, that would be just daft – but he knew Lara could both understand and read. Ben explained to Sophie and Ollie how they could communicate with Lara by asking a series of 'yes' and 'no' questions. 'She can't speak, but she can understand. She will shake or nod if you ask "yes" or "no" questions. Try it.'

Sophie composed herself and tried to think of a question to ask. 'Lara, are you special?' she began.

Nod.

Sophie glanced up at her brother, to see him grinning just as much as she was.

'Can you understand me?'

Vigorous nod.

'Can you understand Ben?'

Very big nod. Lara looked at Ben and winked.

'Can you understand Ollie?'

Shrug that meant: *Sometimes, but he does talk some rubbish*.

'Why are you special? Oh no, you can't answer that because you can't talk. Erm, are you allowed to let grown-ups know you're special?'

Big shake of the head. *Certainly not, or they'd get me on the telly, and then the baddies might come after me.*

'Can you whistle?'

Not half. Get a load of this. Lara pursed her doggy lips, stood on her hind legs and composed herself before breaking into a dance routine, her paws tapping out a rhythm while she whistled along with the tune. The remarkable show ended with a curtsy and some kisses blown to an imaginary audience. *There's more,* thought Lara, *lots more, but I don't want to show off too much.*

Ben and Sophie didn't see it as showing

off, they just watched with pride. This was their dog – and look what she could do!

'We all love you, Lara. You know that, don't you? You're part of the family.'

Nod.

'Do you love us?'

Big nod.

'How much?'

Lara stood on her hind legs and spread her front paws as wide as they would go, like an angler exaggerating the size of his catch. *That much*, thought Lara, *and more besides*.

'Are you going to be our dog forever?'

Lara nodded, although inwardly she was more uncertain. *Certainly that's my hope*, she thought. *I just pray I can keep my promise.*

16. *A Holiday Adventure*

It was on the morning of the Cooks' last day on holiday that the real action began. Dad was up first. He let Lara out for a wee and then proceeded to gather the ingredients together for a cooked breakfast. 'Come on, you lazy lot!' he yelled. 'This is our last day of holiday and we've got lots to do. I want to cram in a last surf, cliff walk, swim and cream tea. And it all needs to start with a holiday-style breakfast. Hurry, or we won't be able to squeeze everything in.'

The rest of the family surfaced, more slowly than Dad, but gradually warming to his enthusiasm.

'We need some eggs to go in the fry-up,' he told Ben. 'Take some money out of Mum's purse and pop to the farm shop. Take

Lara with you – oh, and your brother and sister too.'

Ben, Sophie and Ollie dragged their clothes on, the same clothes they'd had on yesterday, but that didn't seem to matter so much on holiday. Sophie was keen to get the eggs so Dad could do his special fried ones, exactly how she liked them: crispy underbellies and soft, yellow yolks. Dad was the best at eggs.

They found Lara sniffing for rabbits on the hillside beside their cottage. 'Come on, La La!' shouted Ollie. 'We've got eggs to fetch.'

Lara bounded up to the children and then on ahead, lolloping along, nose to the ground. She was enjoying just being a dog with no special responsibilities and no VIPs to protect.

The path from the cottage took them along a typically narrow Devon lane, down a steep hill, to Mrs George's farm shop. The views on the way were spectacular: a huge sandy bay several miles long, with blue sky and a vast, shimmering sea with one or two early-morning surfers hoping to be the first to catch a big wave.

Ben held Ollie's hand as they went into Mrs George's shop. The lady behind the counter greeted them warmly. 'Oh, hello again, you guys,' she beamed. 'What's Dad sent you for this time – eggs, bread, milk, bacon, or everything?'

'Just eggs, please, Mrs George,' said Ben, holding out a ten-pound note.

'It's your last day today, isn't it?' said the lady sadly. 'I bet you'll be taking this lovely weather back to the Midlands with you. Tell your dad there's no charge for the eggs, so long as you all promise to come back again next year.'

'Promise,' chorused the children together,

taking the half-dozen freshly laid eggs and thanking Mrs George.

'Let's just go down the hill to the beach and watch the surfers for a minute or two,' suggested Ben as they left the shop.

The children turned right out of the farm and headed down the hill towards the beach. They hadn't quite got there when they heard excited, urgent shouting coming from someone on the beach. Ben took Ollie's hand and broke into a trot. Sensing danger, Lara was already sprinting ahead.

'My little boys have been blown out to sea in their dinghy,' squealed a woman, pointing

out into the vast expanse of sea. The children could just make out a small rubber dinghy, far out on the water, much too far away to swim. 'I only took my eyes off them for a minute, and they've gone all that way out, and neither of them can swim very well,' gasped the lady, who was getting herself into an awful state.

One of the surfers reached into his beach bag and pulled out his mobile, ringing 999 and requesting coastguard assistance. Lara figured it would be quite a while before the coastguard arrived, so she would take action now.

Ben looked at Lara. Lara looked at Ben. 'Is this going to be another of your missions?' he asked the dog.

Lara nodded solemnly.

'What do you need me to do?'

Lara nosed in the surfer's bag, pulling out a snorkel and goggles.

'I can't swim all that way, you silly dog,' said Ben, pointing to the dot of a dinghy on the horizon.

Lara shook her head wildly, stood on her hind legs and pointed at herself, jabbing her paw into her barrel chest.

'What, *you* want to wear the snorkel and goggles so you can rescue the kids?' gasped Ben.

This is better than Scooby-Doo, thought Lara, nodding frantically. *I can make myself perfectly understood after all!*

Ben struggled to get the goggles and snorkel on to Lara. It was quite a painful experience because they didn't fit well and he kept trapping Lara's fur in the goggles' strap. While the adults stood and gazed helplessly out to sea, Lara sped into the water, goggles on and snorkel clenched in her jaws. She had practised this before, but never very successfully; still, now it was the real thing so she had to get it right.

Lara splashed through the first few icy waves and then, legs pumping like mad, she plunged into the deep water. She knew from her swimming instructor that the doggy paddle was slow and inefficient. She glided along smoothly, snorkel clenched in her teeth, doing her best front crawl.

Mum and Dad heard the commotion and came out of the clifftop cottage. They stood, rooted to the spot, and watched the action unfolding on the beach below. They could clearly make out a snorkelling dog, head down in the water with one ear raised above the waves. Even from that distance the ear was unmistakable.

'Sophie was right, she *is* special. Get a load of that front crawl!' gasped Dad, quite unable to believe his eyes.

Lara kicked her legs furiously. On the surface she was gliding along, but the energy and action was all taking place below. She got closer to the boys and held her head out of the water. She gave a half bark, which was all she could manage with the snorkel in her jaws. The boys had lost a paddle and one of them was leaning dangerously far out of the dinghy, trying to reach the floating oar. With a big splash (and a terrified distant scream from their mum on shore), the boy toppled into the deep blue ocean. His mum was right: he couldn't swim very well at all.

Lara had to swim even quicker, her legs kicking harder and her breathing getting shorter. The boy was going under, then coming back to the surface, gasping for air.

His gasps were getting shorter – there wasn't much time.

Lara reached the boy in the dinghy, who looked faintly surprised to see a dog wearing goggles and so far out in the ocean. He pointed to the spot where he had last seen his brother. 'He's in there, doggie,' said the boy, pointing earnestly to the calm surface of the sea.

No sign of the boy at all, he must be sinking, thought Lara, *so here goes.* She spat the snorkel out, took a deep, doggy breath, filling her lungs with as much oxygen as possible, and dived under the water. All was quiet beneath the surface, except for the pumping of her heart and the bubbles she blew as she sank deeper and deeper in search of the boy. It got darker the deeper she went, and she was glad of the goggles, as they made it much easier to see, even though the poor fit meant they were already half full of salt water. She twizzled round in the water, doing a complete circle, trying to find the sinking child. There he was, down a bit further to her right, still flapping his arms like a flightless bird. His face registered

panic – not at the sight of an underwater spy dog with flapping ears and Speedo goggles, but at the fact that his breath and life were slipping away.

Lara's lungs were beginning to hurt. Pumping her legs meant she was running dangerously low on oxygen, but she wouldn't get a second chance. Everything seemed to be moving in slow motion. She started doing breast stroke in order to go even deeper, figuring that if she returned to the surface to refuel her lungs, the boy would be gone forever.

She used her last supplies of oxygen to reach the boy, whose eyes were wide with panic, his limbs weakening and his body about to give up. Lara grabbed his collar in her teeth and, using every bit of effort, began to haul him to the surface. It seemed desperately slow and painful. He was a dead weight and she had no power left in her legs. But she had to do it, there was no choice – if she couldn't do it, it couldn't be done.

Eventually Lara surfaced, letting go of the boy for a moment while she took in a huge lungful of fresh air. Then she grabbed him again and towed him towards the dinghy. As she did so, a coastguard helicopter arrived, hovering noisily overhead, churning the ocean into a frenzy of wind and waves. *For goodness' sake*, thought the bedraggled dog, *you're making matters worse, not better.*

Lara couldn't get the boy back into the dinghy. His brother was in shock, sitting silent and still, oblivious to what was going on and unable to help pull his brother aboard.

The helicopter let down a winch and a lifeguard was lowered to hoist the unconscious boy aboard. The lifeguard and boy were winched to safety and the helicopter flew off, returning the sea to its tranquil state.

A motorboat pulled alongside Lara, and a sturdy man reached into the ocean and yanked the dog on-board by her collar. She lay, coughing and spluttering, seawater bubbles churning up from her stomach. She was wet through and exhausted, but she had rescued the boy.

A few minutes later, the lifeboat landed on the beach and everyone applauded and cheered Lara as she stumbled off the boat on to dry land. Ben and Sophie ran to her and hugged her, dropping the eggs and getting sodden in the process.

Ollie hung back, taking it all in his stride, explaining proudly to onlookers that she also did karate and could whistle. Mum and Dad had reached the beach to welcome Lara on to dry land, after watching most of the adventure from the clifftop.

The day never calmed down. By the time all the reporters and wellwishers had left, it was bedtime and Dad had arranged with Mrs George that they would stay an extra night, returning home the following morning.

Lara was a true hero. *To be honest, it was hardly 'blending into the background', but what choice did I have? The boy would have drowned. I had to do it.*

The story didn't just make the local news, it spread as far as the national news. Mum, Dad, Ben and Lara stayed up to watch the footage shot from the rescue helicopter, which clearly showed a black-and-white dog, one ear up and one ear down, rescuing a drowning boy from the sea. It was a genuinely uplifting news story and was included at the end of the bulletin, in the 'Good News' section. The newsreader finished by saying that both boys were expected to make a full recovery. 'That's some dog.' He smiled to his co-presenter as they cut to the weather update.

'Too right,' howled Dad, punching the air. 'Did you see that, Lara? That was you, on the news. You're going to be a star. Everyone's going to want to meet you. You're going to be famous!'

That's exactly what worries me, Lara thought. She was in two minds about the coverage. On the one hand, she was proud to have used her training in such a good way. She was a hero, and that felt good. On the other hand, she was now totally exposed on national TV. If Mr Big wanted to get to her, he knew who she was, where she was and which family she belonged to. It was possible that they were all now in danger.

17. *Closing In*

Professor Cortex poured the hot milk into his cocoa and stirred in a heaped teaspoon of his home-made brain formula. He yawned. He had endured yet another fruitless day of searching. His team had visited twenty-four houses that day and had brought eight black-and-white dogs back to headquarters for identification – all negative. He and his team had now checked every dog rescue shelter within a hundred-mile radius and he was beginning to get worried. It might well turn his remaining three hairs white. Could GM451 be dead? It seemed to be the only logical explanation. There was just one more house to check – the one where the old lady had called the police – the one that had cost him a night behind bars! There had been no sign of the family, so the house was being watched, just in case. His bad temper and exhaustion were made worse by having stayed up half the previous night, explaining his story to the police. His whole team had spent the night in the cells while the police checked out his far-fetched story about spies and super dogs. Eventually the boss of the spy agency had been summoned from her bed and the matter was sorted out, but not before much apologizing and embarrassment.

The professor flicked on the TV, hoping to catch the news at ten. He sat in his favourite armchair and stirred his cocoa.

Blast, he'd missed the news again, it was just coming to an end.

'And finally,' announced the newsreader, 'what about this for a daring rescue by a heroic dog . . .'

The mug of cocoa dropped to the floor, staining the carpet, as the professor watched the news open-mouthed. There she was, on primetime TV, clear as day.

'That's some dog,' said the presenter.

'Some dog indeed,' echoed the professor.

'Blend into the background. Just be a normal dog,' he muttered. 'GM451, what have you done?'

The criminal in the ripped designer suit was also watching the news, standing up because his buttocks were still too sore for him to think about sitting. He was not at all surprised by Lara's exploits because he knew her true capabilities only too well. After all, she'd used all her skills and knowledge to bring his drug-smuggling empire crashing to the ground. That dog had spied on his gang, learnt his secrets and then turned them over to the British police. It had cost him billions of pounds, his homes in Miami, Barbados and Monaco, his yacht; in fact, all the ill-gotten gains he'd built up over the years were now gone – thanks to that dog. Super dog they were calling her. Dead dog more like.

Thanks to the news, he now knew who and where she was. He could hardly sleep that night. He was so looking forward to finally getting his hands on the spy dog.

18. *In for the Kill*

It was a long drive home from Devon. Everyone, especially Lara, was exhausted, and they drove quietly, with the children snoozing in the back. Sophie was snuggled up with her pillow and Ollie crashed out in his booster seat, mouth wide open. Even Ben was flat out, worn out by the excitement of the sea rescue and his late night.

They approached home and Dad drove the car into the drive and pulled on the handbrake. The neighbourhood was as peaceful as ever, quite a contrast to the excitement of the last couple of days. Ben woke up, but his brother and sister were still fast asleep, so Mum decided to let them snooze a little longer. Dad opened the boot to let Lara out while Mum disappeared upstairs to start unpacking the cases and sorting out dirty clothes into various piles for washing.

Mr Big had been waiting all morning. His car was parked a short distance down the road and he'd watched the Cooks' car enter the driveway in his rear-view mirror. He reached into the glove compartment for his leather gloves, pulling them once again over his scarred hands. He put his gun in his jacket pocket and stepped purposefully out of the car.

The Secret Service man had been parked a short distance in the other direction. He too had been waiting all morning – in fact, since 4 a.m. His stomach had been telling him he'd missed breakfast. Two minutes before the Cooks arrived, he had driven off in search of something to eat.

Mr Big approached the house. He glanced at the two children, still fast asleep in the car. There was no sign of the spy dog. He approached the house and banged on the door – even his knock was evil.

Lara was slurping water from her bowl in

the kitchen and looked up to see Dad heading for the door. She heard him open it.

'Hi,' Lara heard him say. 'What can we do for you?'

Lara stopped slurping and listened. 'It's about your dog,' the man said. 'I saw her on TV and I think she might be the dog that I used to have.'

They've come to collect me, panicked Lara. *Professor Cortex and the Secret Service team have finally tracked me down.* Her heart sank. She was desperate to stay with the children. She adored them and they adored her. She always knew the Secret Service would find her and it wasn't many weeks before that she had been longing to be rescued. But that was before she'd tasted the love of a family. Although she knew it was bound to happen, it didn't make it any easier to accept.

Maybe if I hide, they'll get fed up and go away and I'll be allowed to stay? she thought desperately. It was worth a try. Lara glanced around the kitchen, looking for somewhere to conceal herself. There was only one place. She climbed into the nearby wicker linen basket that Mum had brought down from

upstairs. Lara pulled the lid down and hid herself among the dirty clothes. There were some strange smells (especially, she noticed, from Dad's socks) but it made a good hiding place. She was able to peep out through the small gaps in the wickerwork. It was ideal: she could see out but others couldn't see in – perfect for spying.

Dad had continued his conversation on the doorstep, oblivious to the fact that he was talking to an armed drug baron who was intent on getting revenge on the dog that had ruined his criminal empire.

'Oh,' Lara heard Dad say sadly, 'I don't know where we stand, because we adopted Lara from the RSPCA. The kids love her. Well, to be honest, we all do, and we'd hate to lose her . . . but I suppose if she's yours . . .?'

Dad's mind was racing. How would he explain this to Ben and Sophie? They would be terribly upset, so would Ollie, and so, come to think of it, would Mum. 'You'd better come in and sit down,' Dad offered, opening the door to let the man through.

'Thanks,' said the man. 'I'll come in and stand up, if that's OK?'

The two men went through to the kitchen, where Lara watched them from the security of the linen basket.

'I'll go and find her for you,' Dad suggested. 'She's probably digging holes in the garden.'

But, of course, Lara wasn't in the garden, she was cowering in the linen basket, full of fear when she saw who this man was. She recognized the voice, but even more his distinctive smell, and she remembered the taste of his fleshy bottom. She knew instinctively that this man would stop at nothing. He would get rid of the whole family if need be. She had to come up with a plan, and quickly. *Think, Lara, think. And keep that heart quiet, it's thumping like a drum!*

She heard Dad calling for her in the garden but she kept absolutely still and quiet, within spitting distance of the baddie, concealed in the basket with Dad's dirty socks on her nose. She could just make the man out through the gaps. She smiled to herself as she watched him feeling his bottom, gingerly moving his hand from buttock to buttock, wincing as he did. Then her jaw dropped in horror as he opened his jacket and patted the revolver reassuringly.

This is the worst possible situation, thought Lara. *A Grade One alert.*

Dad came back into the kitchen. 'Can't seem to find her anywhere,' he said truthfully. 'She was here a minute ago, but she seems to have gone walkabout.' He spotted a dirty tea towel on the floor and picked it up. Lara held her breath as he approached the linen basket. She cringed, waiting for him to open it and reveal her hiding place.

'I must have her, she's very dear to me,' lied Mr Big.

Dad hovered by the linen basket. He had an uneasy feeling. There was something about this man that didn't ring true. Why, for instance, did he have a heavy coat on in the middle of summer, and those leather gloves?

Dad decided to ask a few more questions. 'Where did you get Lara from?' he enquired in a passing-the-time-of-day kind of way.

'Erm, erm,' stammered the man, 'probably a pet shop, I should think.'

Liar, thought Dad. 'And when was that?'

'Oh, a long time ago – after all, she's getting on a bit now, isn't she?' he continued unconvincingly.

No, thought Dad, *she's only three and if you had owned her you would know that*. He lifted the basket lid, holding it open while he thought about his next question. Neither man noticed one black-and-white ear poking out of the top. Lara stopped breathing and shut her eyes tight, expecting to be noticed at any moment.

'Oh, right,' said Dad. 'And did you buy her that engraved blue collar she wears?'

'Of course. She's had that since she was a puppy,' lied the man. 'Look, enough of the small talk, I need to know where she is. I need to take her home today, *now* even.'

Now Dad knew he was lying. Lara had a red collar, not a blue one. If he were really her owner, he would surely know that. Why was he lying? And why did he want to take Lara away?

'Tell you what,' suggested Dad. 'Leave your phone number and we'll call you when Lara gets in. She could be anywhere, you could be waiting ages.' Dad threw the tea towel into the basket and shut the lid.

Lara breathed a huge but silent sigh of relief.

'I'm taking the mutt today,' said the drug baron. 'I think this will help convince you I'm not kidding. Perhaps it will focus your mind?'

'Consider me focused,' stammered Dad, eyes wide with terror, staring down the barrel of the revolver that the man had pulled from his jacket pocket. 'Focused entirely, never been more focused, not ever,' he repeated, mesmerized by the gun.

Lara's heart was thumping. She considered her options, of which there weren't many. She could leap out and try to take the gun from Mr Big, but she reckoned on a 99 per cent chance of failure. After all, it took only a fraction of a second to pull the trigger, so she and Dad could well end up dead – not a great option. Or she could sit tight and wait, which for now was more appealing.

'Come with me and search for this menace of a dog,' ordered the man, shunting Dad forward with the muzzle of his gun. Dad walked stiffly out into the garden, fearful for the safety of himself and his family.

After the two men had left the kitchen, Lara stood up and poked her head out of the basket, a comical sight with one ear up, one ear down, a tea towel on her head and Dad's dirty socks hanging from her nose. *Pooey!* She checked that the coast was clear then wobbled the basket until it tipped over. She crept silently out. *What to do next? The priority has to be to the safety of the children, two of whom are still in the car.*

Lara tiptoed quietly through the hallway just as Ben came galloping down the stairs. 'There you are, Lara,' he shouted. 'I've been looking for you everywhere. Do you want to come outside for a game of footy?'

Lara cringed and put her paw across her

lips to signify 'shush'. *Quiet, stop, don't go that way, there's a killer in the back garden.*

But Ben didn't get the message. He skipped through the kitchen, making for the back door. 'Come on, Lara,' he called, 'let's go and play football outsi–' Before he could finish his sentence he'd been brought crashing to the ground. Lara had rugby tackled him. *Sorry, Ben, but it's the only way I can think of shutting you up.*

The boy was confused. He was being expertly pinned to the ground by a furry rugby player. Lara seemed to have changed. Her eyes were wild and there was a warning growl coming from her throat. *This is a Grade One alert. Set foot outside and we're goners. Please understand.*

'What's up, Lara?' he asked nervously. 'I want to play football, not rugby.'

If you want to live to play football again, then follow me, she urged, hauling him to his feet and tugging him towards the front door. Ben had no choice but to be dragged outside on to the drive.

Lara ran to the car and jumped into the driver's seat, beckoning Ben to join her. She pointed to the key. *Turn it, please*, she urged. *Please understand. It is so important that we escape. I have to get you away from this house as quickly as possible.*

'You want to drive the car?' Ben laughed. 'You've got to be joking, Lara. I mean, I know you can do some clever tricks, but driving a car?'

At that moment Mr Big poked his head out of an upstairs window. 'Oi, mutt. Stop right there.' Ben and Lara looked up to see a man waving a gun, pointing it in their direction. Ben looked at Lara, who just shrugged. *See what I mean? This is no joke.*

Now Ben understood. He immediately reached into the car and turned the key, sparking the engine into life. He ran round to the passenger side and jumped in, buckling up and casting an eye over his shoulder to check on his sister and brother, still asleep in the back. 'You can drive, can't you, Lara?' he asked hesitantly. She nodded, hiding the whole truth. *Well, it's a bit difficult with paws instead of hands, but with your help we might be OK.* She quickly surveyed the car's controls, familiarizing herself with the basics.

Excellent, it's an automatic, so no awkward gears to mess with. She nudged the lever into 'reverse' and stretched for the accelerator. *So far so good.*

Mr Big came running out of the house, gun held out in front of him. Lara and Ben saw him coming, then glanced at each other, their eyes saying it all.

Lara stamped hard on the accelerator pedal. The engine screamed but the car stayed put. Smoke started billowing from the tyres. *Oh, this is so difficult. Why aren't we moving?*

'The handbrake, Lara. You've got to let the handbrake off,' yelled Ben. 'Like this,' he said, releasing the brake. The car shot backwards, bounced out of the drive and across the road, and smashed through Gran's fence. *Whoops, sorry, old girl*, thought Lara, stamping on the brake.

The jolt woke Sophie and Ollie. 'Are we nearly home, Dad?' croaked Sophie in a half-awake, half-asleep state.

'Woof,' came the rather surprising answer from the driver's seat.

Woof? thought Sophie, coming to full consciousness very quickly. 'Oh my goodness,' she wailed, alarming Ollie with a faint scream. 'Lara's driving the car.'

Ollie came round quickly, roused by the panic in his sister's voice. He was sitting directly behind the driver's seat, and instead of seeing Dad's head in front he spied one ear up and one down. He was less panicky, taking a driving dog pretty much in his stride. 'Clever dog, Lara,' he observed. 'Cool driving, 'specially for a dog. But why are we in Gran's garden?'

Ben tried to reassure the others. 'No idea what's going on,' he shouted over his shoulder, 'but I think it's one of Lara's adventures. Seatbelts on and hold tight!'

Lara knocked the lever into 'drive' and floored the accelerator once more, wheel-spinning the car across the lawn. She was at full stretch, struggling to reach the pedals and steer at the same time. *This will have to be a team effort*, she thought. *I'll concentrate on the pedals if you help steer.* Ben was already leaning over, wrestling with the steering wheel, crunching the car over Gran's fence and out on to the main road.

Mr Big and Dad chased the vehicle on to the road and Mum popped her head out of the bathroom window to see Lara in semi-control of the family car, indicating right but turning left on to the main road, windscreen wipers at full speed despite the sunny weather.

The parents were in a panic because the children were in danger, and Mr Big was panicking because his arch-enemy, that dratted spy dog, was escaping. He raced to his car, leapt in, revved the engine and added to the stench of burning rubber, wheel-spinning his car in hot pursuit.

The Secret Service man drove back from his burger breakfast just in time to see Lara mount the kerb and disappear round the corner, with Mr Big in hot pursuit. He dropped down a gear and joined the chase.

Gran was walking back from the shops when the first car sped by. Ben was doing brilliantly with the steering, his hours spent on the PlayStation rally games finally paying off. Gran recognized the car and waved. Lara was at full stretch in the driver's seat, legs extended to the pedals. She smiled and waved back, trying to look as calm and casual as a driving dog can. Gran's jaw dropped, as did her shopping – apples and oranges rolled into the road.

Moments later, Mr Big's car roared by, squashing the apples flat and exploding the oranges, soaking Gran's ankles in vitamin C. The old lady rubbed her eyes in disbelief. *It must be old age*, she thought, *dogs can't possibly drive cars!* She made a mental note to make an appointment to get her eyes tested. The old lady composed herself, and then bent down to rescue her carton of milk from the side of the road just as the Secret Service car roared by, exploding the milk carton and soaking Gran from head to foot. She removed her milky glasses and shook her head. What with driving dogs and then boy racers, she was having a bad day.

But Lara could certainly drive – admittedly not very well, but she was doing her best. With Ben's help she headed left, then right, swinging the car dangerously round the corners, trying to avoid other motorists on the way. Horns were blaring and tyres screeching; pedestrians jumped out of the way, shaking their fists in anger and then shaking their heads in disbelief when they saw who was driving.

Lara glanced in the rear-view mirror. The other car was getting closer all the time. Lara was giving her all but she couldn't take too many risks with the children in the car, so she had to keep the speed fairly low. They turned right again, into North Street, heading towards the police station. *Please let there be a policeman on duty.*

Sophie was terrified. She knew that Lara

was special, but she wasn't certain about her driving. Ollie stretched his neck to look out of the rear window. 'There's a car chasing us,' he announced, remarkably calmly. He looked again, this time more urgently. 'And it's catching us up really quickly.'

I know, panicked Lara. *But I daren't go any faster.*

There was no sound of a bullet, but the back window of the car shattered into a million pieces as the first shot hit. Lara floored the accelerator, the engine screaming, the temperature gauge rising. *Nearly there, nearly at the police station. But then what? It's me he wants, not the kids, so think, Lara, think.*

The rear tyres blew, first one then the other. *He's a great shot.* Ben couldn't control the steering any longer. They mounted the kerb and smashed through a dustbin, a trail of rubbish billowing after the car. 'We've got to stop, Lara!' he shouted. 'We'll have to give up.'

Lara ploughed on. *No chance. Giving up is not an option. Not much further to the police station. We have to give it our best shot.* The tyres had gone, the metal rims were causing sparks to fly from the wheels. The car demolished another bin, before lurching back on to the road. Ben and Lara continued to wrestle the steering wheel, desperately trying to avoid oncoming traffic. Mr Big's car came alongside them. Lara glanced across and saw him grinning. He's enjoying himself, she thought. He's a complete madman. He swerved into Lara's car, trying to force her off the road. There was a crash of metal as the cars came together, but Ben held on tight and kept the car pointing in the right direction. Mr Big overtook them and swung his car across the road, blocking their way. Lara slammed her foot on the brake in an emergency stop. She shot forward and banged her nose on the steering wheel. Luckily the children were strapped in.

Now there can be no plan, just action. My first priority has to be the children. Do whatever it takes, but get him away from the children. Lara used her teeth to pull out the keys and leapt from the car, pressing the central locking button, securing the children safely inside. She ran for her life. It was now her versus the armed villain, just as before, only this time the odds seemed even worse. The children's faces appeared at the window, screaming silently. *Stay down, kids. For goodness' sake keep your heads down*, she barked.

Mr Big jumped from his vehicle, wincing at the pain in his bottom, pulling the pistol from his car. Lara leapt at him: he shot

wildly, in blind panic, remembering the sharpness of her jaws from the last time they met. The first bullet missed, just whizzing past Lara's left ear, embedding itself in a wheelie bin. The second hit, going clean through her upright ear, making a perfectly round hole. *Ouch, that hurt.* The third one hit too, more seriously, in her right shoulder. *Now that really hurt, a lot.*

She couldn't remember the fourth or fifth, although they also hit her. But Lara did remember grabbing the man's hand and sinking her teeth in, making him drop the gun; but after that, nothing – just blackness.

19. *No Laughing Matter*

It wasn't until five days later that Lara finally awoke. She was lying on a couch which, by the smell of it, was in some sort of hospital, probably a vet's. She tried to move but was consumed by pain in her shoulder, leg and foot.

Ben and Sophie were there, by her side. They had taken it in turns to be with their pet, stroking the sleeping animal.

'Lara, you're awake,' whispered Ben excitedly. 'Look, Sophie, she's opened her eyes. I knew you would wake up. The vet said you might not, but I knew you would. How do you feel? Oh no, you can't answer that. Erm, does it hurt?'

Lara nodded gravely. *Even nodding hurts!*

'Where does it hurt most?' he enquired.

Lara lifted her one good paw and pointed to just about everywhere. *Here, here, here, and especially here.*

'Oh, you poor mutt,' said Ben. 'The police say you got shot five times by that horrible man. You've got a hole in your ear and one of the bullets is still in you. The vet says it's safer to leave it in than take it out. But you will get better, won't you? Please promise.'

Lara nodded painfully. *I certainly hope so.*

'Does it really, really hurt?' asked Sophie.

Only when I laugh. She smiled, closing her eyes and drifting off into another deep sleep.

20. *Duty Calls*

Lara was left to recuperate, returning to the Cooks' house ten days later, still limping and in pain, but very much on the mend. She arrived to a hero's welcome. Mum had even baked her a cake in the shape of a bone.

Ben had kept the newspaper cuttings for Lara to read. It seemed that the Secret Service agent had arrived just in time to tackle Mr Big as he dropped the gun. The baddie was now safely in prison and was expected to stay there for a very long time.

Just desserts for such a horrible man, thought Lara.

Lara recovered slowly, with Ben and Sophie tending to her every wish – although, to be honest, her only wish was to get better and to be able to stay with her family.

It was three days later that Dad took the call. Lara knew that it would come and she knew from the look on Dad's face that she was being called back to the Secret Service.

Lara was very sad. The children were even sadder. Ben couldn't care less about setting a good example. He yelled and sobbed. 'It's so unfair. She's family, Dad. She wants to stay and we want her to stay, so why can't she?'

Sophie, so often the grown-up young lady, sobbed like a little girl and she seemed permanently misty-eyed and red-faced. Nobody could console her.

Ollie couldn't understand why Lara had to go. 'Who am I going to play computer games with?' he asked.

The children and Lara spent their last day working on their football skills and then having a picnic. Sophie helped Lara make her favourite sandwiches – salami and banana – but none of them was really hungry.

On Lara's final night she was allowed to sleep at the foot of Ben's bed and, when Mum and Dad had switched off the light, he allowed his pet to snuggle under the duvet.

★

The Secret Service team were due at ten o'clock the next morning and, typically when you don't want it to, the time was flying by. The children had a few minutes alone with Lara while the clock sped towards the allotted hour.

None of them knew what to say, but it was Ollie who broke the ice. 'I love you, Lara, and I really don't want you to go. Can I come with you?' he asked.

A sad shake of the head. Lara was very upset. She desperately wanted to stay. She couldn't cope with being taken away from the family, and especially from the children she loved. Her doleful, doggy eyes were sad; her big doggy heart was heavy.

'Maybe we can visit you?' suggested Ben bravely. 'You must have weekends off or something. Maybe you could put yourself on a train and come and see us?' A glimmer of hope struck up in his voice.

Lara tried to smile and she nodded unconvincingly. She knew visits were unlikely, as her job meant that she could be sent anywhere in the world and that, once again, everything she did would be a secret.

The Secret Service van drew up in the drive. Several special agents jumped out, all dressed in identical black suits and shades. Professor Cortex was the last to emerge, smoothing his three grey hairs across his scalp before approaching the house. He knocked on the door and came straight in. 'Good morning, GM451,' he said. 'You have made a full recovery, I hope?'

It's all matter-of-fact and there's no love. I don't want to go back to this, but I have no choice. Lara nodded sadly. *My body may recover, but I don't think my feelings ever will.*

The family pet licked Mum, then Dad, and sat and shook paws with Ollie, who solemnly presented her with the blue ball. All three had tears streaming down their faces at the loss of their beloved Lara.

Lara jumped up on to her hind legs and walked over to Sophie. They had a last cuddle, paws on shoulders and arms round the dog's waist. Sophie squeezed so tight so that it made Lara wince in pain, but she didn't mind – the pain in her heart was worse. Sophie cried big tears until her T-shirt was soaked.

Finally Lara approached Ben, who was trying so hard to be brave. He was ten and didn't like to show his feelings, but his watery smile was fed by a steady trickle of tears. They shook hands and saluted each other, as cool as could be, before embracing, and the trickle becoming a flood.

Finally it was time to go. As if to emphasize her special status, Lara jumped into the front passenger seat of the Secret Service van, put on her sunglasses and buckled her seatbelt. The electric window glided down and the spy dog blew a kiss to the family. She gave a farewell woof. *You're the best family I could have chosen. I'm going to miss you all so much. So very much.*

The van drove off and all the family waved as Lara left them to continue her secret government work.

21. *A Special Assembly*

Nobody spoke for the rest of the day. Dad went for a very long walk. Mum and Sophie were completely choked with tears. It just didn't seem right that Lara had been taken away. Ollie played on his PlayStation, but it wasn't so much fun without Lara. Ben retreated into silent mode. Life was just so unfair.

'Perhaps we can get another dog?' suggested Dad, making matters worse. There were no other dogs that the children wanted. Everyone moped for the next day, and the one after that.

On the third day, Dad took a call in his upstairs office. After the call, Mum and Dad seemed to perk up. Ben and Sophie remained as heartbroken as ever and couldn't believe how their parents could be so cheerful when such an awful thing had happened.

Monday came and everyone went their separate ways – Dad and Mum to work, Ollie to nursery and the older children to school. Not that the children felt like it, but Mum insisted.

Everyone at school knew about Lara – after all, she'd been on the local and national news, and was a real celebrity. Children swarmed around Ben, asking questions and saying how proud they were to have had such a clever dog in their neighbourhood. Ben just about managed to maintain his composure, while his younger sister erupted into floods of tears.

A special assembly was called, and all the classes gathered in the school hall. For some reason, Dad was up on the stage, along with the head teacher, Mr Bell.

What's Dad doing here? mouthed Ben to his tearful sister across the hall. Sophie shrugged.

Mr Bell asked for quiet, and a hush fell on the hall.

'As you all know, Mr Cook and his family

have recently had quite an adventure. I'm sure you have all been following it in the news.' There were enthusiastic nods and whispers from the assembled crowd of children before Mr Bell waved his arms for more quiet, and the muttering subsided.

'Their special dog, Lara, rescued a drowning boy. It's also been revealed that she captured some criminals on the industrial estate and then rescued Mr Cook's children from a man with a gun. It was a terrible, terrible situation. Really terrible,' emphasized Mr Bell, struggling for words other than 'terrible'. 'The poor dog was shot, and then it turned out she was a special dog and had to be returned to the government. She was a spy dog, doing good for the world. Sadly, she had to go back into training. I know Ben and Sophie are very sad.'

Tears were welling up again in Ben's eyes. He glanced across at his sister, who was sobbing loudly. *Yes, we are very sad indeed, thanks, but why a special assembly? Surely it couldn't be . . .* He hardly dared think it.

As if reading Ben's mind, Mr Bell continued, 'However, Lara doesn't want to go back into the Secret Service, she would much rather stay with the Cooks. What's more, her owner, Professor Cortex, says she isn't now fit enough to work for them. She was shot five times and still has a bullet lodged in her thigh. She's not as fast or as fit as she was before the shooting.'

Sophie's tears had stopped. Hope had replaced the heaviness in her heart. She brushed away the wetness with her sleeve and sniffed the slime back up her nose. She began to look a little more like her usual self and glanced across at her brother, who was focusing on Dad.

Dad was beaming from ear to ear. Ben smiled weakly back at him, still unsure what was going on, afraid to believe what he was hearing.

'So,' continued Mr Bell triumphantly, 'it has been decided that Lara can come back and stay in our neighbourhood, making us all a lot safer. Mr Cook and his family are going to get Lara back —'

There was more, but Ben and Sophie didn't hear it. Lara had bounded on to the stage, to the cheers of 613 school children,

the restrained yelling of one ten-year-old boy and the excited squealing of one little girl.

The spy dog stood proudly on stage, one ear down and one standing up, clear daylight showing through the bullet hole.

Ben and Sophie ran to the front and threw their arms round Lara's neck. Lara licked them furiously, as if they were melting ice creams that needed tidying up quickly. She tasted the remains of a week's worth of tears that had flowed down the children's faces.

No need for any more of that, she thought, *this time I'm here to stay.*